City of the Dead

The Vendetta Saga, Volume 3

Arianna Courson

Published by Arianna Courson, 2024.

This is a work of fiction. Similarities to real people, places, or events are entirely coincidental.

CITY OF THE DEAD

First edition. November 3, 2024.

Copyright © 2024 Arianna Courson.

ISBN: 979-8224090051

Written by Arianna Courson.

Also by Arianna Courson

Chronicles of the Enchanted
The Silent Kiss
The Silent Kiss
Lullaby: A Book of Enchanted Shorts

The Bane Saga
Alpha Bane

The Chained Saga
Quiet, Now
Quiet, Now
Be Still
Be Still

The Crave Saga
Crave

Chains
Secrets
Bloodless: The Entire Crave Saga

The Fallen Shadow Saga
Lily's Fallen Shadow
Jason's Angel of Storms
Silence Me
Silence Me

The Vendetta Saga
The Demon's Duchess
The Shattered Carnival
City of the Dead
The Wonderland Show
A Song of Darkness
Duchess of Death
Vendetta

Standalone
Obsession
Catch Me if You Can
Catch Me if You Can
Corrupted
The Eleventh Hour

Table of Contents

Act III – City of the Dead 1
Introducing Part 18 – Little Spy 3
1 5
2 13
Introducing Part 19 – Rich and Rude 19
3 21
Introducing Part 20 – The Culprit 37
4 39
Introducing Part 21 - Manslaughter 45
5 47
Introducing Part 22 – Murder on the Urge 55
6 57
Introducing Part 23 – He's Not Dead 67
7 69
8 71
Introducing Part 24 – Victim Number Five 83
9 85
Introducing Part 25 – Movement in the Shadows 91
10 93
Introducing Part 26 – A Second Attempt 99
11 101
Introducing Part 27 – Knowing the Culprit 111
12 113
Introducing Part 28 – Done with Waiting 135
13 137

to my mother

Act III – City of the Dead

xxxxxxxxxxxxxxxxxxxxxxxxxxx

Introducing Part 18 – Little Spy

C*hapters 1 – 2*

1

Alistair
Little Spy

I stared down at the fork I was currently polishing, lashes lowered as I quietly set it aside and moved to another one.

It was about one in the morning, and since duchess was asleep, I always did the tidying and small little chores at this time of night. Sleeping wasn't necessary for a demon like me, anyway.

As I quietly moved onto a spoon, a shadow moved behind me.

I just smiled, setting the spoon aside and moving onto a butterknife. "Out of bed again, duchess?"

There was no response.

I kept polishing. "I know you're hiding behind the pantry door, my lady. You should know by now that sneaking around me in hopes I won't notice isn't possible."

There was still no response.

I just sighed and set the knife down, immediately turning and stepping over to the pantry door.

I then moved it forward, finding Hazel pressed against the wall.

She gazed up in surprise, clearly thinking that I was stalling.

She was still in her nightshirt, the buttoned cloth going down to her knees, but her eye patch was gone, exposing the glistening rune in her right eye.

"Duchess, this is the third time this week," I said as she glared at me. "When are you actually going to stay in bed and sleep?"

She just made an impatient sound. "I slept long enough."

"Three hours isn't long enough."

"I don't particularly care," she said then, looking up at me. "You made me mad!"

"Oh?" I arched a brow, still smiling.

She just puffed her cheek in annoyance, still glaring. "You were... supposed to stay."

My lashes lowered. "Duchess, I have chores to do at night."

"Any normal person would sleep at night," she argued.

"Ah," I said then, "but I'm not normal, am I?"

"Indeed, so you can get the chores done during the day," she said, gazing up at me. "Admit it, you just do these chores at night to pass the time."

"And if I am?"

She looked taken aback for a moment, and then looked away. "You were supposed to stay."

"Are you mad that I left your room?" I said, chuckling. "My, you're growing very attached to me, aren't you?"

"Shut it."

"Why don't you go back to bed?" I said, lightly pushing her out from the corner. "You need your rest. I have stuff I have to do, alright?"

She just made an impatient sound and left the room, going back down the hall.

I just smiled after her. "Something tells me this isn't the last I'll see of you tonight." I just chuckled and turned back to my tasks. "I want to see how desperate you'll become."

Thirty minutes later, I waved off the cloth of the dining table and replaced it with a new one, finishing by stretching out the wrinkles and brushing it down evenly.

But I just stood and smiled, patting off my hands before I stepped over to the window on the far right of the wall.

I pulled back the curtains, finding Hazel standing there with her cheeks slightly shaded.

She gazed up in surprise.

I pointed to the direction of her room. "Bed."

She grumbled in annoyance and stepped off back to her bedroom, and I just smiled after her.

Twenty minutes after that, I arranged the black roses in the main entrance, fixing them correctly in their pots.

I then sighed and shook my head, stepping over to a pillar and peering behind it.

Of course, Hazel was crouching behind it.

She looked angrier now that I found her.

I just arched a brow, knowing that she understood my silent command.

She just grumbled and stood, going back to her bedroom.

It was about four in the morning now, and I was dusting off the staircase in the main entrance, making sure I got every corner.

"Duchess," I said then, "bed."

She walked out from a corner wall behind me and sighed, going back upstairs.

I gazed up at her in amusement when she passed me, and then went back to my chores.

It was eight in the morning now, and Hazel hadn't left her bedroom since four this morning.

But... despite her being a stubborn child and spying on me all night, I knew it was time to wake her up. Or at least... check to make sure she was in her bedroom.

I briefly knocked on the bedroom door, holding her tray of chai in my hand. "Duchess, it's me."

There was no response.

I just opened the door, walking further in the room.

But when I locked eyes with her bed, I blinked when I found it empty.

I sighed then. "Of course she's not here. Why would she be?"

I then turned and gazed further in the house, scanning the rooms for her presence.

Scarlet... Cammie... Carter... Maddox...

They were all still in bed, of course, but where was duchess?

I blinked when I sensed her, and I stared in that direction. "Why are you in there?"

I then closed her bedroom door and stepped down the hall, making my way down to the main level before turning and going down to the basement.

I then continued down the quiet halls before I stopped at my bedroom door.

Was she snooping again? Of course, she was. What else would she be doing?

I then knocked. "Duchess, I know you're in there."

There was no response.

I just sighed and opened the door, gazing around for her presence.

I blinked then, lips parting.

Hazel was on my bed, snuggled under the covers and asleep, her head pressed to my pillow as she breathed softly.

The covers were puffed around her, and her lashes were glistening under the small amount of morning sun that cast through the windows.

My lashes lowered as I smiled. "Very needy, indeed."

I just closed the door behind me and set the chai on a table by my bed, stepping over to her as she remained sound asleep.

I then sat on the bed, pulling some of her hair away from her face. "Duchess."

She groaned in annoyance and turned her face further into the pillow.

"Still tired?" I said, chuckling. "You see, this is what happens when you refuse to sleep at night."

She just pulled the covers higher over herself and turned away, clearly trying to sleep longer.

I just watched her for a moment, and I smiled gently.

I just kicked off my shoes and lowered myself onto the bed beside her, got under the covers, and watched her curiously.

But I decided to bother her and pulled her shoulder, so she faced me.

She kicked out her legs in annoyance and whined like a child, but I just pulled her against me and wrapped my arms around her.

She stopped fighting then, clearly half-asleep right now.

After a moment, she settled in my grip, burying her face in my shoulder as I smiled.

I just pulled the covers higher over her. "Twenty more minutes, okay?"

She never responded, clearly lost in those dreams of hers.

"Duchess," I said as she took a bite of her eggs, reading the newspaper, "may I ask why you were sleeping in my bed last night?"

She dropped the newspaper and sent me a look. "Because I was tired, and I didn't know the direction of my bedroom."

I smiled at her horrible attempt at a lie. "Really? So, you didn't notice yourself going down two sets of stairs and then down the hall, specifically to my bedroom?"

She glared.

"You could've entered Carter's, or Cammie's, or Scarlet's, but you sought fit to enter mine out of random circumstances?" I said then, smile widening. "Especially when you spied on me all night because you were lonely and wanted my presence?"

She looked back down at her paper. "I don't appreciate you accusing me of things, Alistair."

I closed my eyes and smiled. "I do apologize, but I can't help but mention that you have a massive amount of confidence, but you're very adorable, my lady. You're like a small little bunny that wants to be held."

She lowered the paper and sent me a warning look.

"But my reasoning is," I continued, "I have very a high suspicion that you were feeling very needy last night, and I was busy, so you slept in my bed because it smelled like me."

She just dropped the newspaper, giving me a very sharp glare. "Your comments are infuriating. Shut it, Alistair."

I just parted my eyes and bowed. "At once, my lady."

She grumbled in annoyance and kept reading her newspaper.

"Aliissssssssttttaiiiiiirrr!" Scarlet said, running out from the hallway. "Heeeeeeeeelp!"

I sighed and gazed up. "What did you do now?"

She just waved her hands quickly. "Maddox blew up the kitchen!"

"Again?" I said, brows arching. "That's the sixth time this *week*."

Hazel just smiled, sipping her chai lightly. "Better get on with it, Alistair."

I looked down at her in annoyance. "You enjoy my misery, don't you, duchess?"

"I would be lying if I said no." She gazed up at me in amusement.

I just sighed and looked over at Scarlet. "I swear you hired these children just to inconvenience me, my lady."

She just laughed silently.

I stepped over to Scarlet. "Alright, show me to the mess."

2

Hazel
Little Spy (Continued)

"Duchess," Maddox said as the last two servants entered the room, "you called?"

I gazed up and nodded as Alistair remained at my side, smiling with his eyes closed. "Indeed, I did."

"What happened, duchess?" Cammie said, brows drawing together. "Did something come up?"

"As a matter of fact, it did," I said, setting my elbows on my desk, "but if the question is if it's good or bad, that is up to you." I looked up at them then. "How do you four feel about a vacation?"

Cammie's eyes widened immediately, and Scarlet squealed, jumping in elation.

"You're shitting me," Carter said then, and Maddox puffed his cheeks to conceal his excitement.

"Carter," Alistair said calmly, "what did I say about explicit language in front of our duchess?"

He immediately stiffened. "Shit! Fuck! Sorry...."

I had to avoid smiling. "Anyways, I assume you all are for going on vacation?"

"I love the idea!" Scarlet said, waving her hands excitedly.

"But where to, duchess?" Cammie said then, the only one remaining calm.

"Well," I said, sighing as I set my cheek in my hand, "my family owns many businesses on land like factories for children's clothes and soaps. But, I realized, that there is no business at sea. So, I thought about maybe starting a yacht line, where I can sell yachts to people." I tapped my fingers on my desk. "Of course, I'd have to buy one first and test it out in order to completely understand the aspects of marketing yacht-line material."

"We're going on a ship?" Maddox said, eyes sparkling like a child. "Really, duchess?"

"Indeed," I said then, gazing up with a sly smile, "I purchased a yacht for us and a few others. Sadly, the ship has others on it as well, but it is people we know, so it isn't over-crowded." I pursed my lips. "None of you get sea sickness, do you?"

"How can we kill with such a weakness?" all of them said at once.

I smiled then. "Of course, I apologize for doubting."

"Alright, now that you're told, pack your bags," Alistair said then, clapping his hands. "Chop, chop. We are leaving tonight."

They all skittered from the room.

"In *my* opinion," I said, sighing as my lashes lowered, "vacations sound boring. I wish something interesting were to happen. Relaxing just isn't my thing."

Alistair gazed down at me and smiled, eyes glowing slightly.

"My, duchess," Alistair said as we all gazed up at the ship in front of us, "how did you manage paying for something this large? It's very big, indeed, and can hold so many people. Must you have paid extra for lesser people, my lady? Isn't the point of this to get the word out?"

I made an impatient sound as the horn sounded, all of us starting toward the staircase that lead to the main dock. "I hate people. I would pay a million dollars if I had to."

Alistair and the four other servants followed behind me. "Duchess, you sure have your priorities mixed up, don't you?"

"Alistair, you have been smack-talking me for the last ten days now." I glared over at him. "I am your duchess, stop it."

He just closed his eyes, bowing slightly when we made it to the main dock. "My apologies, my lady."

"All aboard!" the captain called, waving toward the last amount of guests entering the ship.

"All aboard?" Cammie echoed. "This is a ship, not a train."

"'Ey," Carter said, "let 'em workers have some fun, aight? They're probably treated like shit by these rich folk."

I gazed over at him then, brows arching.

He immediately shrank back, throwing his hands up innocently. "No offense to you, duchess! I was not trying to offend you in the slightest! You saved a homeless lad like me, 'member?"

"No, you're right," I said then, closing my eyes and smiling. "I do treat people like shit. It's one of my favorite tasks. Especially to my caretaker. Right, Alistair?"

He just smirked down at me. "Assuredly, my lady." He then looked over at Carter in annoyance. "The explicit *language*, Carter."

He immediately paled and bowed quickly. "Fuck, sorry!"

I just chuckled.

The horns on the boat blasted through the air, and suddenly, we started moving.

I toppled over slightly, but Alistair caught my arm.

"Careful, duchess," he said then, smiling. "You wouldn't look good as a floor mat."

I gave him a look.

He just chuckled.

But—all the sudden—a man bumped into my back, making me stumble again when Alistair caught me to help me steady.

I looked back, annoyed, but the man suddenly glanced down at me, making me blink when I saw him wearing a large, tan trench coat and a fedora of the same color. Small specks of his hair peaked out from his hat, colored a dark black.

He just smiled. "My apologies, young lady. My balance seems a bit off."

He then walked off.

Alistair immediately shot his eyes to look after him, lashes lowering in suspicion.

I watched his red irises glow as if he was suddenly angry.

"What is it?" I said then, glancing over at what he was looking at.

Alistair watched as the man vanished into the small crowd. "That's unfortunate."

My brows drew together in question.

He just gazed down at me. "Duchess, I'd advise that you stay close to me. It is simply a command."

"Why?" I said then, brows drawing together.

Alistair just closed his eyes and smiled. "It's just simply a beg, duchess. Stay close, please."

I just narrowed my eyes at him. "Alright, whatever."

Alistair just gazed down at me, smiling. "You wanted this to be more interesting because you feared it'd be boring. Well, duchess, I would say that since *he's* here, things are going to be very interesting, indeed."

I arched a brow. "Who's he?"

"Well, if I told you, this game wouldn't be fun, would it?"

Introducing Part 19 – Rich and Rude

C*hapter 3*

3

Hazel
Rich and Rude

"Ow! Hey! Stop it!" I yelled when Alistair tightened the strings of my corset. "That hurts, you idiot!"

He just smiled and tied the front into a bow. "My apologies, duchess. I was just trying to get it to stay, that's all."

"You're such a liar," I hissed when he pulled my arms through the sleeves of my dress. "You enjoy my misery."

"Ah, no, I cannot lie, duchess, remember?" he said then, buttoning my dress. "You told me to never lie to you. But I will admit, watching you fume is very adorable."

I glared at him. "I'll hit you."

"I'll dodge you."

"I will make it hurt."

He gazed up then, smiling. "Are you seriously saying that to a demon? The strongest human on Earth can punch me and all it would do is itch."

I arched a brow. "Then why are you dodging it if you're so... *indestructible*?"

"Good question, my lady," he said, standing and catching my jacket. "And you'll never know the answer."

21

"Whatever," I said then, rolling my eyes as he guided the jacket on. "Why must I wear this ugly, itchy thing?"

"You're about to go to a fancy dinner," Alistair stated, brushing down my sleeves. "You must look the part."

"I always look the part!" I argued. "Must you go *this* far?"

He smiled up at me. "My answer remains the same."

I just rolled my eyes. "Whatever. Just... hurry up already."

"I'm already done," he said then, smiling as he stood. "You look lovely now, duchess. Congratulations on surviving the torture."

"I can do without the sarcasm, thank you."

He just parted his lashes and let his red eyes settle on me. "Someone's angry tonight. May I ask why?"

"No, you may not." I closed my eyes and crossed my arms over my chest. "Because you already know the answer."

He just let his lashes flutter shut, the smile still there. "If you hate them so much, why did you invite them?"

"Because I can toy with them," I said, looking up at him now. "It's fun, Alistair. You should know with how many people you toy with before you kill them."

He looked down at me then. "My, my, accusing me of such things?"

"I'm not accusing," I said in boredom, "I'm stating a fact."

He looked more amused than anything. "Well, duchess, it's almost six o'clock. It's time for the dinner."

I groaned in annoyance and buried my face in my hands. "I don't wanna."

"My apologies, duchess, but didn't you just say you liked to toy with them?" He smiled in amusement. "But you're stilling dreading seeing their faces?"

"They're annoying."

"Indeed, they are." He shook his head, chuckling. "And yet you still invited them. Isn't it safe to assume that you keep lying to yourself in hopes to strengthen your self-confidence?"

I threw my head up, glaring. "I don't need personal insight from a *demon*."

"Well, us *demons* are very insightful, indeed." He looked down at me, red eyes glowing dangerously.

"Your amusement is hideous."

"Why, thank you. I appreciate the compliment." He just tipped his head to the side. "If my amusement were adorable, then how can I protect my duchess from horrid things, hmm?"

I gave him a look, but then settled back into myself. "Alistair."

He gazed up. "Yes, my lady?"

"Who was that man?" I said then, lashes lowering. "The one you were clearly suspicious of?"

He just closed his eyes. "Not for you to worry."

I glared then. "Alistair."

"Duchess," he said, tone curt, "the dinner is in two minutes. It's time to go."

I just let my gaze sharpen. "I don't like it when you hide things from me."

"It's in your best interest, my lady." He gazed down, eyes soft. "I promise you that."

"I can demand you to tell me!" I argued then.

He just smiled. "You can. But will you?"

I clenched my teeth and tightened my fists.

"You know there's something going on, yes," Alistair said then, lashes lowering, "but you also understand that I have it covered, don't you? You will not tell me to do something if I think it's not for the best. You understand that I always have a plan in place, and that I will never let you get hurt."

I just lowered my head, body shaking with annoyance.

"It's time for the party, duchess," Alistair said then. "Let's go."

"Hazel!" a girl called, making my lashes lower. "Hello! I missed you so!"

I gazed down at the crowd to find three girls running toward me.

Not these bitches... really? They were the first to greet me?

Alistair was right, I made a mistake inviting them, didn't I?

My three cousins, Kate, Jamison, and Matilda stopped in front of me, bowing like I was suddenly their queen.

"Hello, cuz!" Matilda said way to casually. "It's nice to see you!"

"We're very sorry about last time," Kate expressed frantically. "We were so cruel to you, and we see that now."

"Now, now, girls," Alistair said then, stepping forward.

They all shrank back in fear, stumbling a little as they huddled together. "*Alistair*!" they said together, more out of surprise.

He just smiled kindly. "My duchess needs to greet her other guests, too, so give her some space, alright?"

They all bowed quickly. "At once!" And they rushed off.

I just smiled a little. "You made quite the impression on them."

He just gazed after them curiously, watching them huddle in a corner behind their mother. "It seems I did."

"Yes, well, whatever happens, I shall be safe with your menacing, demonic, black, fire-like shadow behind me."

He just followed after me. "That was a lot of descriptions of me, duchess. If I were smart, I think you were hinting that you were afraid of me."

"Oh, I definitely am," I said, making him blink and gaze down. I just smiled. "You are a demon after all, you were contracted to kill me for the longest time. I would be a fool if I wasn't afraid, wouldn't I?"

He stared at me for a moment, surprised even though I've expressed this before.

But he just smiled, lashes lowering as his eyes glowed dangerously. "And you are no fool, duchess."

"Indeed, I am not." I stopped in front of our guests, Alistair by my side.

"Hello, everyone!" I said in an oddly chipper voice. "My name is Hazel Damonclove, heir to the throne and keeper of the criminals. I am so glad all of you could make it! This is a rare, and oddly occurring circumstance that we're all here, isn't it?" I laughed. "I am anti-social, after all."

They all laughed even though I was serious.

"This is Alistair, my caretaker," I said, gesturing to him.

He bowed before them. "A pleasure to meet your acquaintance."

He stood up when I gestured to my other four servants standing in a corner and adjusting their clothes. "And those are my other servants."

They all shot up, surprised that I introduced them.

"Cammie is the short one with the curly hair, she serves as a maid of my mansion," I said, "and the tall one is Carter, the houseboy. Maddox is the one wearing the fedora, he's the cook for my mansion. And the other girl with the blonde hair is Scarlet, my other maid."

They all bowed simultaneously before standing up straight. "A pleasure."

"Now, if you'll all please introduce yourself to everyone," I said, clapping my hands together. "We'll start with you, over there."

I pointed to my three cousins.

Their cheeks burned a bright red, and they glanced at each other before looking at their mother, my aunt.

Aunt Beth just arched her brows.

They then looked back forward, separating from each other at an instant and closing their eyes kindly.

"I'm Matilda," one of them said, closing her eyes kindly.

"I'm Kate."

"And I'm Jamison! We're all Hazel's cousins!"

"My name is Beth Damonclove," my aunt said then, splaying her hand over her chest as she gazed up. "I am Hazel's aunt, and this is my husband, Minister Curtis."

He nodded, letting out a *hmph* as an agreement.

Another girl piped up then, smiling kindly as the hat she wore topped over with her movement. "My name is Claudia! I am a manager at one of Duchess Hazel's toy factories!"

A man with dark skin and a top hat bowed before me. "I am Jeffery, manager of the perfume department."

"My name is Savage," another girl said, smiling kindly. "An odd name, I know, but I manage the medicinal department."

"I go by Deneise," another woman said, closing her eyes as her smile remained gone. "I manage the floral department."

"And my name is Beham Damonclove," my grandmother said, smiling kindly as she chuckled, "I am old and worn down, but I serve as Hazel's grandmother."

All of them laughed a little at her small joke, and I just smiled.

After a moment, we all looked down to the final guest, lips parting.

It was a cold, emotionless-looking man, and he just gritted his teeth. "Name's Denver," he said then, voice gruff, "weapons department."

I watched him suspiciously before gazing up at the guests. "Thank you all for coming! I appreciate this more than you can imagine. Now, Maddox will guide you all to the dining room just across the hall. If you'll all follow him."

He gazed up in shock then, brows drawing together as he pointed to himself. "*Me*?"

"Yes, you," I said quietly, "go!"

"But I blew up the *kitchen*!"

"All you have to do is *walk*," Carter said then, making me roll my eyes. "And unless you got bombs in those shoes, you'll be fine! I gotcha!"

He just grumbled in protest and started forward, Carter following behind him, making Alistair chuckle a little as Maddox bowed unevenly and gazed up. "If you'll follow me!"

All the guest murmured in amusement as they exited the room and into the dining room.

"Hey, Cammie," Scarlet said then, making us gaze over. "You know... Carter mentioned something about bombs in his shoes...."

"Oh, that was *one time*!" she said then, shaking her head as she glared. "I haven't done it since!"

"Well, you did it *once* which is why I had to ask," Scarlet said then, rolling her eyes.

"It didn't even go *off*! I made sure they were duds."

"Yes, but you still scared the crap out of him."

Cammie gazed up then. "That was the point. He ate my mashed potatoes. I was warning him not to step out of line."

Alistair watched their encounter in amusement.

I just gazed up at him. "I didn't see that guy you were suspicious of. None of the guests looked like him."

"Indeed, you did not." He kept watching Cammie and Scarlet. "But he could be one of the guests."

I just let my lashes lower. "None of them have black hair."

"Ah, but there is a thing called a disguise," he said then, gazing down at me. "But no matter. Come, now. Dinner, my lady."

He then started down the stairs and I followed after him.

"It still could've gone off!" Scarlet said.

"It was a *dud*!" Cammie argued.

"How do you know?!"

"Because I just do!"

"Idiots..." I grumbled, "all of them."

Alistair just smiled.

"Wow, Alistair, where did you get that ass?" Madam Claudia said.

I choked on my water, coughing seconds later.

Alistair just gazed over me at amusement, just finishing with prepping the champagne. "I'm afraid I don't have an answer to that, my lady."

She puffed a cheek and walked off, clearly looking a little annoyed that she was ignored.

Alistair stepped over to me as I kept coughing, kneeling seconds later. "Duchess, why must you inhale water so? It's not good for you."

"*Really?*" I said sarcastically. "I couldn't help but feel a little surprised when I caught you," I continued coughing, "*flirting*."

"Oh, my," he said then, covering his mouth as his lips parted, "is duchess *jealous*?"

I gave him a look. "Shut up, you fiend."

He just chuckled and stood, lightly catching a cloth from a nearby table and dabbing my lips. "You look a mess, duchess." He finished. "There. That's better."

He then stood and tossed the napkin away.

"Hey!" someone said then, making me gaze up in question as the entire room silenced.

Denver just stepped over to that Claudia girl, brows furrowed in anger.

"You bitch!" he snapped then, showing her his champagne cup. "Did you spike my drink?"

She stepped backward then, looking a little nervous. "Why would I do such a thing? And how would you know if it was spiked without drinking it?"

Alistair cleaned off his hands and continued with adjusting everything back in place, so it looked nice.

Denver just took a menacing step forward. "Don't play games with me! That odd girl over there drank it and looks in pieces!"

We all gazed over to find Scarlet wobbling around. "It's alright," she said, slurring her words. "The carpenter said it would be cheesecake."

Great. Now I had this mess on my hands.

Denver took a menacing step toward Claudia. "I asked a question!"

"I did not spike your drink!" she yelled. "Why would I do that?"

"You're jealous of me, admit it!" he said then, glaring. "Ever since I broke up with you, you've been stalking me endlessly!"

"I don't know what you're talking about!" she yelled back.

He just shoved his drink forward, the champagne splaying out and coming straight toward her.

She gazed up in surprise.

But I moved faster.

I shoved myself in front of her, making him gaze up in surprise as the liquid came down upon me, splashing me in seconds.

Everyone gasped, shrinking backwards in confusion.

"Did he just splash Duchess...?" one guest said.

"I think he just did."

"But she's just a child," another whispered.

I gazed up then, champagne dripping off my bangs and splashing onto the floor. "Now, now, Sir Denver," I said, lashes lowering in annoyance. "Is that any way to treat a lady?"

He immediately gritted his teeth, glaring down at me. "Hey! This is all on you! You stepped in front of this bitch in the first place!"

I lowered my head, looking into his eyes deeply. "No matter what she did to you," I said, voice low so only he could hear, "humiliating her in front of an audience is cruel, don't you think? Especially knowing that it was you who spiked the drink in the first place, hoping to pin it on her."

He glared sharply, raising his hand that held the glass. "You don't know anything, you little brat!"

He then brought the glass down onto me, making the people in the room gasp.

But his arm was caught from a sudden figure before it could come close to hitting me.

He gazed up then, eyes widening when he saw the man.

Alistair stood there, holding onto his wrist tightly. "Please do not attempt to harm my duchess," he said, smiling as his eyes glowed a dark red. "You already doused her in alcohol. Isn't that enough?"

"Did you see him move...?" a girl whispered, gazing behind her to a faraway table. "Wasn't he just over there?"

"Maybe he moved," another responded. "I don't know."

Denver pulled his arm then, and Alistair let go, watching him stumble backward.

He just gritted his teeth and stormed off, tossing his glass in the trash can.

"Ah, so wasteful," Alistair remarked, watching him leave to go to his room. "Very heartless, if you ask me. Those glasses were expensive, too."

"Leave him be," I said then, shaking my head to rid of some of the liquid from my hair. "He's a jerk, not a monster."

I then looked over to the crowd. "I apologize for the disturbance, everyone. Please, continue enjoying your meals, alright?"

They all murmured in agreement and went back to what they were doing.

I gazed up at Alistair then, finding him raising a towel that he got from God knew where, and he lightly set it on my head, rubbing my hair.

"You're going to mess up my hair, Alistair," I said then.

"It's already messed up," he argued. "And relax, duchess. It's almost time for bed, anyway. You reek of alcohol. If there was an officer here, you might be arrested for underage drinking."

"Ha, ha," I said sarcastically, "very funny."

"I am hilarious, I know," he said then, lightly going down to rubbing my shoulders and neck. "My," he said quietly, "you're soaked." His lashes lowered. "What a cruel man."

"Don't touch him," I said then, voice soft so no one else could hear. "I mean it. I wouldn't know how to explain his disappearance. We're on a ship, after all."

Alistair just nodded gently. "Indeed, my lady. I will not."

"And everything's so insane now-a-days!" Matilda said frantically as we stood in the billiard room together. "Don't you think, Claudia?"

The girl just nodded numbly. "Indeed." She paused, blinking as if she'd been spacing out the whole time. "What were we talking about again?"

Matilda gave her an annoyed look, and I just rolled my eyes and checked my watch, finding the hour hand ticking past eleven.

"Hey, do you know where mom is?" Aunt Beth said then, gazing around. "She's been gone for a while."

"Maybe she's with the others," Minister Curtis said then, sipping his coffee.

I just arched my brows.

Was it really time for coffee? It was almost midnight... did this man sleep?

Curtis just lowered his drink. "I heard that the others decided to stay over at the dining hall together to finish the appetizers."

"Ugh, pigs," Beth said then, scoffing. "Seriously."

I gazed over at Alistair then, finding him cleaning a glass with a cloth. "Is it time to retire?"

He set the glass aside and gazed up. "Indeed, it is, my lady."

I nodded and looked up at the few guests in the room. "Alright, everyone! I shall return to my chambers for the night. It was nice spending time with you."

Aunt Beth just gave me a bored look at my kindness, but I ignored it.

"Actually, I'm tired, too," Matilda said then, yawning as she stretched out her arms.

"Yeah, all that arguing exhausted me to my core," Claudia mentioned, shoulders slumping.

"I guess I can retire," Aunt Beth said, gazing over at Curtis and his coffee. "Not sure about him, though."

"Oh, I can just sit in bed and stare at the ceiling all night," Curtis said then, shrugging. "No problem."

"Way to sound so sane, dad," Matilda remarked.

He just gave her a look.

"Alright, whatever," I said then, turning and starting out the door and they followed behind me. "I guess the halls are all the same, so I'm stuck with everyone, aren't I?"

"How unfortunate for your antisocial tendencies, my lady," Alistair said then.

I gave him an annoyed look and he just smiled.

"Oh, cuz!" Matilda said, rushing after me before stopping at my side.

She gave Alistair a nervous glance before looking down at me. "Hi. Can I ask you something?"

"Is it tedious?" I remarked.

"I don't think so."

"Then ask. I haven't got all night."

She swallowed something hard and leaned forward. "Uhm... about Alistair. Has he... you know... killed people?"

I gazed over at her then. "He drinks blood. What do you think?"

Her face paled immediately as she gazed up at him, clearly to see if he was listening.

He was, though, staring down at her with his eyes glowing a dark red.

Her entire form whitened, and she scrambled backward, clearly in attempt to get away.

"You could've lied to her, my lady," Alistair said then.

"What fun is that?" I smiled a little. "I didn't lie nor tell the truth, anyway. I merely hinted the answer."

He just smiled and gazed forward, and we all continued walking together.

He immediately stopped then, holding out his arm to make me, as well.

I bumped into it before I could react, and then gazed up at him. "What?"

The others slowed behind us, glancing around nervously.

Alistair narrowed his eyes. "Duchess. Look ahead."

I just blinked before gazed over to see what he was suspicious of.

My entire being froze.

A man lay crumpled on the hallway floor, eyes rolled to the top of his head as his breaths remained silent.

Blood spread among the entire carpet, clearly coming from a wound on his chest.

My breath shook as my eyes widened, frost covering my entire form.

Alistair just sniffed the air, lashes lowering. "It smells like almonds," he said out of nowhere.

I felt my fingers twitch at my sides when I recognized the victim's pupilless gold eyes and short, blonde hair from anywhere.

The man murdered in the hallway of this ship...

Sir Denver.

Introducing Part 20 – The Culprit

Chapter 4

4

Hazel
The Culprit

"Everyone," Alistair said calmly, raising his hands slightly and pushed them forward, "settle down."

"Settle *down*?" Matilda echoed. "One of us was *murdered*! Are you insane?!"

"How can we *settle down* knowing that there's a killer on this ship?!" Aunt Beth retorted, cheeks burning red in fear. "This is complete and utter chaos!"

"Everybody!" I yelled then. "If you want to live, we must remain *calm*!"

The entire room silenced then, and everyone settled in their seats, breaths straining.

"Now, we must assess the situation like normal," I stated, lashes lowering. "There are no detectives on this ship but me, so we must be clear and precise when examining the situation. Madam Beth is a doctor, so she assessed the body and determined the death as a stabbing straight to the heart. Knowing this is the first step, but the next plausible thing to do is ask for alibis."

The room silenced for a moment, but Aunt Beth spoke up first. "I was in the room with you, Hazel! And Curtis, Matilda, Claudia, and Alistair!"

"I was with Sir Jeffery, Madam Deneise, and those two girls over there," Madam Savage said, pointing to my other two cousins. "We were finishing off the dinner platters."

"And us four servants were all washing up in the kitchen!" Maddox said then, brows drawing together.

We all were silent for a moment, and I pressed my finger to my chin, thinking.

But then my eyes widened, and we all gazed over to Madam Beham—my grandmother—who sat on the chair casually.

"Mom?" Madam Beth said then, brows drawing together as Beham sipped her chai casually. "You were the only one alone last night. We were looking for you. Was it you?"

She continued sipping her chai, her pinky pointed outward. "I had no reason to kill that man."

"He splashed your granddaughter and then threatened to hit her!" Sir Jeffery said then, glaring. "That's plenty motive to me."

"Yes, I do see your point," Madam Beham said then, "but I don't have anger outbursts like that."

"How are we supposed to *believe* you?" Deneise said then, glaring. "You could be full of shit."

My lashes lowered then, and my lips thinned when I recalled the man earlier today:

Sorry about that. I can be clumsy sometimes.

I narrowed my eyes then, now thinking of my words:

I didn't see that man today. He's not one of them.

And then Alistair's:

People can be a master of disguise, my lady.

I then gazed up.

If Alistair was so suspicious of that man, then there was a ninety percent chance that he was the murderer.

If he was, the killer... was male.

Although none of the men were alone at the time of Denver's death, which proved my theory wrong.

So, there was another ten percent chance that I was wrong.

"I think it better if we all went to bed," I said then, lashes lowering. "I will team one of my servants up with Madam Beham to assure that she will not kill again."

Even though there was little chance she would murder out of hatred, and I truly disbelieved that she would kill.

"Which servant is up for some prisoner watching?" I said then, gazing around.

Cammie and Scarlet raised their hands.

"Fine, then," I said, looking over to Beham. "You will be chained to one of my servants until we get to land or prove your innocence."

Beham just set her cup aside and gazed up at me, smiling softly. "If that's what will take to ease everyone's minds, then I guess I'll do it."

Cammie just reached under a table and pulled out some chains from an escape route, cuffing herself before walking over to Madam Beham and sliding the second cuff over her wrist. "I'll do it, Scarlet," Cammie said then, gazing over. "You can sleep peacefully tonight."

Scarlet bowed. "I appreciate your kindness."

We all then gazed around before I smiled. "Well, it's time for bed. Good night, everyone."

"What about the murderer?"

"She's chained to a very skilled servant," Alistair said then, voice oddly calm. "Cammie's an expert at self-defense. She'll be fine."

Everyone just murmured in response and gave me a scared look before exiting the room.

After the dining hall doors closed behind them, I gazed up at grandmother.

"You're very bright, Hazel," she said, smiling slightly. "I'll give you that."

My lashes lowered. "I'll figure it out, mama."

"I know you will," she said then, gazing up. "You always do. As for him," she said then, gazing up at Alistair, "I hope you are very high on alert. Your duchess's life is in danger, after all."

He nodded. "I know."

"And stay calm," she said, smiling, "even though you already are."

I blinked and gazed over at him, finding his lashes lowering.

That was a hint, wasn't it?

"Good night, Alistair." She waved. "And my lovely granddaughter."

Twenty minutes later, I was sitting on my bed, watching Alistair unclip my shoes and slide them off, readying me for bed.

"Everything about this doesn't make sense," I told him as he slipped off my socks. "The murder, the person being the culprit. I know my grandmother, and although I do not underestimate things, I know that she couldn't have been the killer."

"And why is that?" Alistair said then.

"Madam Beham was the lead of our family before my father," I explained. "She is highly intelligent, skilled, and knows her way of manipulation. If she wanted to kill someone for any reason," my lashes lowered, "then she would've covered her tracks. Just like I do. She would not be a suspect in the slightest." Alistair undid my corset and released the strain against my chest. "She was framed," I said, "I know it."

"Perhaps that is true," Alistair said, sliding my nightshirt over my shoulders. "But there is no other person who could've committed the crime, after all."

I watched him carefully. "Was it you?"

Alistair smiled as he buttoned my shirt. "Why would you accuse me of such things?"

"You're a demon," I stated then, "you have super speed. Let alone your intelligence that is higher than the *smartest computer*. It would only make sense if everyone had an alibi. Not only that, but you were resentful after what he did to me."

Alistair brushed down the wrinkles of my shirt. "All that would be correct, my lady. I could've killed him all while everyone thought I was in the room. Although," he gazed up, "you told me not to."

I blinked then, lips parting.

"I did not kill Sir Denver," Alistair stated gently, "I was not involved in the murder or killing of Sir Denver, either. And you know I cannot lie."

My lashes lowered then, and I looked to the bed as he drew back the sheets.

I crawled under them and gazed up, finding his eyes soft as he pulled the covers over me.

"Good night, my lady." He then started to the door.

"Alistair," I said then, making him stop in his tracks. I just thinned my lips. "Fix this."

His lips curled then, but he kept his back to me. "Yes, duchess."

He then left the room, leaving me in darkness.

Introducing Part 21 - Manslaughter

*C*hapter 5

5

Hazel
Manslaughter

"Duchess!" Cammie cried, slamming open my bedroom door as I shot awake. "Duchess, hurry!"

I stared at her for a moment, breaths shaking at being startled so quickly.

But I scrambled off the bed and rushed toward her. "What is it?"

"Scarlet!" she sobbed. "Hurry!"

My brows drew together, and I rushed down the hall, controlling my breathing as I followed her.

We rounded the corner and entered the dining room, slowing to a stop.

My eyes immediately rounded.

Scarlet lay on the dining room floor, eyes wide open in surprise. Blood splattered all over from a wound on her chest, covering her whitened gown red.

I covered my mouth then, breaths straining.

Alistair was already in the corner of the room, lashes lowered as he stared at her body.

Everyone else was here, too. Everyone except Sir Denver.

Madam Beth had her face paled, watching the body at her feet.

"What is happening?!" Matilda cried.

"It wasn't Madam Beham," Cammie stated, brows drawn together. "She was with me all night!"

"And I was in duchess's bedroom all night," Alistair stated.

They all gave him a questionable glance.

He just arched his brows, seeming too calm right now. "She was having a nightmare. I calmed her."

"Did you leave the room at all last night?" Madam Beth said, eyes narrowing.

"I did once," Alistair stated honestly, "at about midnight. But her body is fresh, she was murdered within the last two hours. And I made it back to duchess's bedroom at twelve thirty last night. I was in the rest of the time."

"Why did you leave?" Madam Savage demanded.

He gazed over at her. "Duchess said to get some more information on the murder, so I was looking around for it."

"Did you find anything?" Savage wondered then.

His lashes lowered, and he bowed his head in defeat.

He found nothing, or at least he was portraying it.

I watched him carefully, wondering why he was still so calm right now.

I mean... he always was. But when his duchess was in danger, he was on alert.

He had been, though. Ever since that guy showed up, the one he refused to tell me about. He looked about as alert as he was then. Maybe this was him trying to mask his fear.

"How do we know if you're telling the truth?!" Madam Beth said then.

"He is!" Maddox butted in. "I saw him! He went into Duchess's room at twelve thirty and hadn't left since!"

"You were out all night?" Beth retorted.

"Yeah," Sir Jeffery said then, "he, Carter, Claudia, and I were walking around and drinking. Having some boring conversations, I'm telling ya. We didn't realize it was seven in the morning by the time we were done."

I just pinched my brows together. "How much alcohol did you consume to lose track of time like that?"

"Lots," Carter said then, setting his head against the wall, "living on pain killers right now with this hangover. All of us are."

All of them nodded at once.

"And Madam Beham was with me all night," Cammie said. "She didn't move once!"

"I can atone to that," Savage said then, gazing over at us. "I slept on the floor of their room to make sure Beham wouldn't leave."

"Deneise, Matilda, and I were together in the same room!" Cousin Kate said then, throwing her arms frantically. "Matilda and I always sleep together when we have nightmares, and Deneise heard us talking, so she came in because she couldn't sleep either!"

I just sighed and pinched the bridge of my nose, breathing uneasily before gazing up. "You know who that leaves?"

I pointed straight over to two women standing at the end of the room. "Madam Beth and Lady Jamison."

Both of their faces paled.

"I would *never*!" Beth stated frantically.

"Why would I kill a lowly *servant*?" Jamison retorted.

Alistair just looked over at her in warning.

She shrank behind her mother then, whimpering.

"Surely you can't think it's *us*!" Beth said, shaking her head. "What use would I have for doing such a thing?"

"Everyone has motives deep inside," I stated then, lashes lowering. "The question is if others can sense it, or if you're very good at hiding it."

Manipulation is a very good tactic, something that us Damoncloves have great power with.

"It wasn't me!" Jamison said then, shaking her head. "I would never do such a thing!"

Straight out of her mother's mouth. Wow.

Like mother, like daughter, I guess.

I sighed in annoyance.

"Here's an idea," Savage said then, raising a finger. "Why don't we check the video surveillance."

"I apologize, madam, but there is none," Alistair said, tone dark. "We just bought this ship two days ago and sailed out a day later. We didn't have time to add surveillance systems."

"How dumb *are* you?" Aunt Beth yelled.

I just gazed over at her. "Well, I didn't think there would be a *murder* happening on my vacation. It doesn't seem like a common occurrence among average people."

I am not average, but still.

"So... let me get this straight," Sir Jeffery said, putting his hands out. "Both murders were relatively similar. Both were stabbings. But everyone on this ship had an alibi for the first, except for Madam Beham, and everyone had one for the second except for Lady Jamison and Madam Beth. Ruling Madam Beham out for the second one, but also ruling Madam Beth and Madam Jamison for the first."

"This all isn't adding up," Madam Savage said then, shaking her head, "what other possibilities could be out there?"

"Two separate murderers?" Sir Jeffery suggested. "It's the only explanation."

"Well, both murders were similar," Deneise said then. "Stabbings! Why would a second murder copy off the first?"

"Because they work together?" Jeffery said weakly.

"Well, it would make sense, but what would they get out of it?" she continued. "It's incredibly hard to copy the first person's act. They had the same weapon, a knife of a certain length, and they knew to aim directly toward the middle of the heart. Why go through the trouble of replicating someone?"

"Maybe they wanted to frame someone!" Lady Jamison stated.

"But, if that was the case, then they would've framed the same person, not someone different. That would overcomplicate things rather than keeping it simple," Deneise said.

"They wouldn't be working together," Sir Jeffery finished. "Because they would be rivals in this situation."

"Exactly!" Deneise said then. "And what do you mean it's the only option? The other thing we can argue is that there's someone else on this ship. Someone that's not us."

Alistair and I immediately glanced at each other.

"You could be very correct, Madam Deneise," Alistair said then, smiling gently. "That would make complete sense. He could be trying to frame someone and overcomplicate things. Playing with us."

"Well... where else could he be?" Sir Jeffery said then.

"Hiding in the shadows," Cousin Kate said, "duh."

"What can we do?" Deneise said then, voice dark. "If he's that good at hiding, then where would we find him?"

"We can look around for clues," Kate stated. "Then we could find him."

"That won't do good," I said then, closing my eyes.

Everyone looked over at me in question.

I just gazed up; eyes dark. "I counted each and every single person on this ship. There was only one other figure that I haven't seen yet, but the number of people on this ship add up to when I counted."

Their brows drew together.

"The only other people on this yacht are everyone in this room," I said, "the deceased, and the captain as well as his assistant who are running the ship."

"Can't we just go to land?!" Jamison cried. "Surely the police can do something about it! Someone told the captain last night, right? To go back to shore?"

"I did. We are very far from land, I'm afraid," Alistair said then, voice thin. "Very far, indeed. It will take about three days to get to the nearest port."

"Really...?" Deneise said then, brows arching. "We've only been gone for forty hours, and we're three days out from land itself?"

"The murder happened last night!" Kate said then. "And another this morning! What are we going to do?"

"What if they kill the captain?" Matilda said, shaking her head. "Are we going to be stranded at sea forever?"

"That would be stupid on the murderer's part," I said then, sighing. "Killing their only way of escaping."

"Duchess has a point," Cammie said then. "After Alistair looked over everyone's credentials with duchess—so she could understand conversations better—no one here has experience with driving a boat. That would be a bad plan for the murderer. It's perfect to assume the captain is safe."

Everyone sighed in relief.

I gazed over at Alistair then before flickering my eyes to the crowd. "We all must stay together, alright? Not one person shall be alone. Is that clear?"

All of them nodded at once.

"Beham, Jamison, Beth," I said, looking over at them. "All of you are suspects and shall be in the same room together with Cammie. She is talented with martial arts and... *other* self-defense mechanisms. Maddox will be with her, too, so she is not targeted."

"Of course, duchess," he and Cammie said together.

I then looked back at the crowd. "We all must keep safe, understand?"

They all nodded at once.

Introducing Part 22 – Murder on the Urge

Chapter 6

6

Hazel
Murder on the Urge

"Duchess," Alistair said as he poured my evening chai, "are you feeling alright? You look pale."

"Do I seem alright?" I asked cynically. "My mind is running in circles."

"Aren't you a little peeved or nervous about Scarlet?" he asked me. "You look awfully calm after a servant's been murdered. Especially with how close you were to her."

I then gazed up at him, lashes lowering.

He watched me back, the red in his irises flowing so easily.

I then arched a brow, tipping my chin up as I raised my hand and signed something to him.

He just closed his eyes and smiled slightly. "I see."

I lowered my lashes, sipping my chai. "Does that answer your question?"

"Indeed, it does." He gazed up. "But if you know who it is, why didn't you just say so?"

"You know why, Alistair," I stated darkly.

He just leaned down to lightly pour my chai back into my cup. "You are very insightful, indeed."

"I'm glad you see me that way," I stated, only half-sarcastically. "Because everyone else is dumber than a two-year-old."

"Aren't you being a little harsh with that sentence, duchess?"

"I am," I said then, sipping my chai. "I will admit that."

"Duchess," Alistair said then, sitting up straighter, "you finished the first piece, knowing the killers. But the second piece is still missing... *the mastermind*. Have you any ideas?"

I set my chai down, lashes lowering. "Ideas, yes, answers, no."

He just stood up straighter and closed his eyes.

"I expect you to fix this, Alistair," I said then.

"I'm handling it," he promised.

I then glanced over at him, just noticing his hair was damp and dripping onto the floor, and his clothes were freshly changed, too. "Why are you *wet*?"

He gazed down at me. "I thought to go for a little swim, that's all."

"Uh, huh," I said sarcastically.

"The dinner tonight's served with freshly grilled lobster and a side of clam chowder, all caught today from the ship's dock by yours truly." Alistair bowed when he finished bragging. "I hope you enjoy."

I stared as everyone cut into their lobster and started eating, having casual conversations with each other as some laughed to mask their fear.

"You caught these yourself?" I said then, shaking my head. "What a demon you are."

"I keep telling you that I am not to be underestimated," Alistair stated proudly.

"Is that why you were wet this morning? You didn't see fit to use a *fishing rod*?"

"What fun is that? I got to swim to the bottom of the ocean where no one has before. It was a very interesting sight indeed. I actually found an angular fish, too." He smiled sweetly. "Sure, it did want to eat me but... predators are predators."

I just rolled my eyes. "Show off."

He just chuckled.

Madam Deneise just sat up, clearing her throat. "Excuse me, everyone. I must go to bed early. I am feeling quite faint, indeed."

She smiled kindly and bowed before everyone, stepping over to the doors that reside behind me.

Right before she made it to the doors, she flipped her hand outward as a small note slipped from her fingers.

I took it silently, and she left the room.

Alistair gazed down at the note before looking up at the crowd. "Is everyone done with their meals?"

All of them nodded at once, and stood from their seats, wiping their mouths.

"Alright," I said then, standing as well, "Carter, you stay back and clean up this mess. Cammie and Maddox with take the suspects to their rooms, and everyone else... make sure you have someone to sleep with tonight, yeah? I don't think another murder would a good sight to see."

They all nodded at once and exited the room.

Cammie sent me a brief look before exiting the room with Beth, Beham, and Jamison.

When they left, I looked up at Carter. "Can you handle this by yourself? Without breaking all the dishes?"

He gave a salute. "Aye, duchess. I can do it!"

"What have I done?" I said as I looked over at Alistair. "What have I done?"

"I know not, duchess," he said, chuckling a little.

I then pulled the note out and gazed down at it, lashes lowering as I read the small, fine text.

I know who the killer is.
Or... the mastermind behind the murders.
These are all but small pranks, she has a real target.
Meet me in my bedroom when everyone's done with dinner. I need to tell you everything with no witnesses.

- Deneise

I immediately clenched the paper in my hand, feeling Alistair gaze down at me in question.

"*Idiot*!" I yelled, immediately rushing out the bedroom door.

I continued down the hall in a hurry, feeling Alistair follow behind me.

"Duchess?" he called. "Duchess, what is it?"

I then stopped at her doorway, brows drawing together when I found an odd thing on the floor.

It was yellow and thin, like a small piece of a blanket.

I picked it up, assessing it thoroughly.

Yarn...?

But I shoved the thought away.

I rushed forward until I met her bedroom, and I immediately slammed open her door.

I froze then, eyes widening as a sudden frost consumed me.

The note slipped from my hands, drifting slowly to the ground.

Alistair stopped behind me, stance immediately stiffening when he saw the dead body lying face-down on the bedroom floor.

Madam Deneise.

"That idiot!" I said, pacing my room frantically. "That moron! What was she thinking?!"

Alistair gazed up as I continued pacing my room. "Duchess, if you'd take a moment to let me know your thoughts, I beg you."

I stopped then, shooting him a look. "You saw the note, don't give me that!" I then pointed to the direction of her room. "She found the mastermind, yes! Something I have yet to do! She found her! She has the evidence! And yet she decides leaving herself alone in her bedroom and waiting for me is the best idea?! Knowing there's a killer on the loose?! That MORON!"

Alistair just lowered his lashes. "You were so calm and collected before, and now you're freaking out."

"This used to be a game," I said then, glaring at him. "Now it's a threat. You know this. You were calm before and now you look as stiff as a statue. You can't hide that from me."

He just kept his gaze to mine. "Duchess, there was no evidence of the murderer in her room. I have a suspicion that her thoughts to you were merely speculation."

"And they were correct," I said then, gazing over at him. "Because if they were not, she wouldn't have been killed."

He remained silent then.

I just closed my eyes tightly. "The murder is getting messy and less planned. Madam Deneise was murdered by stabbing of the brain. The killer hit her in the head with a vase, and it shattered against her head. They then took of the pieces, puncturing one of her eyes all the way through. Immediate death."

Alistair was silent for a moment. "Everyone had an alibi, though. All three suspects were with Cammie and Maddox, everyone else were in each other's rooms. None of this makes sense, I'm afraid."

"Not if there's someone else on the ship," I said then, making his lips part. "Someone that you're suspicious of."

Alistair's lips thinned, and he set his arms against his sides. "Duchess, surely you aren't suggesting that I know the killer."

"Don't you?" I said then, glancing over at him. "You've been on edge, Alistair. I know you have. Who is this mystery man, huh?"

He watched me for a moment but remained silent.

"Fine," I said then, "don't tell me." I then sent him a look. "But you better fix this. I mean it. Find the mastermind, Alistair, and fix this. No matter what it takes."

He bowed before me. "Yes, my lady."

I just made an impatient sound and stepped over to my bed, flopping onto it.

He stepped over to me and knelt down, starting to take off my shoes.

"Duchess," he said quietly, moving onto removing my socks, "please, let me be with you tonight."

I gazed down at him then. "What?"

He just moved to start unbuttoning my shirt. "Allow me to stay tonight. I must keep an eye on you."

I just lowered my lashes, feeling him peel off my dress and slide my night shirt on. "Why are you suddenly protective?"

"I must be," he said then, buttoning the cloth. "My duchess's in danger."

I watched him carefully. "You are asking me for permission, and even so, you and I know very well I cannot say no. This is per the contract's orders."

He smiled then, finishing and gazing up at me. "Look how insightful you are."

"I don't need your sarcasm, Alistair," I said as he pulled the string of my eye patch and let it fall. "We're already down a servant. A *good* one at that. And we're running out of time. I don't know who the killer will target next."

Alistair caught my eye patch and set it on the nightstand. "I will fix this. As per your wishes, my lady." He pulled back the sheets. "But, as for tonight, I must stay."

I just got under the covers, feeling him pull them back over me and stand, blowing out a small candle on my nightstand.

"Why don't you ever use newer technology?" I asked him then.

He just glanced down at me. "I don't like newer technology, duchess."

"It's odd, don't you think…?" I said quietly. "That all the murders don't aim to any person… *person*."

Alistair was silent for a moment, but he just sat on the bed beside me. "I think it's time you go to sleep, duchess."

I gazed up at him then, watching his dark features carefully. But I just snuggled into the pillow. "Sleep with me."

He stared down at me. "Duchess. You know I cannot let my guard down."

"Fine, lay with me." I gazed up.

Why was I doing this?

I was scared, nervous, and felt alone.

I didn't care about judgement anymore. I just wanted a presence.

He just smiled slightly, and he sighed, lowering himself under the covers next to me after kicking off his shoes. "Yes, my lady."

I did something unexpected, though.

I immediately shuffled over to him and snuggled with his chest, making him smile slightly as he ran his fingers through my hair.

"Someone's clingy tonight," he said gently, "are you feeling alright, my lady?"

"Shut up," I said, snuggling closer, "don't ruin this."

He just smiled, chuckling softly. "Alright."

I parted my lashes as he continued brushing his fingers through my hair, staring at his chest lazily. "Do you think that I'm next?"

He suddenly turned toward me and curled himself around me, suddenly very protective. "I will not allow that, duchess. You know I won't."

"I know," I said then, lashes lowering. "What I find odd is that... you were so calm with the first two murders, and now you're stiff and nervous. Why?"

He just buried his face in my hair. "Pardon my rudeness, but you know why, my lady."

I stared at his chest for a moment, and I just closed my eyes. "Perhaps, I do."

He kept me pressed to him but then tightened his hold. "Mine. All mine. You're mine."

My voice was quiet. "I did sell my life to you, after all. So, I am yours, yes..." I then glared at his chest, "no matter how irritating you are every second of my life."

I felt his body rattle with a silent laugh. "You admitted it, duchess."

I slapped his back. "Shut it."

He just chuckled.

Introducing Part 23 – He's Not Dead

Chapters 7 – 8

7

Alistair
He's Not Dead

"Oh, great, look at this mess they made," I said silently, sighing as I lowered myself to my knees and cleaned up the mess on the kitchen floor. "Shattered glass, broken cups. Must duchess have such messy guests?"

I smiled then, chuckling. "It was Carter, wasn't it?"

As I kept cleaning the shards of glass, I finally set them in the trash can, dusting off my hands.

But I gazed up toward the wall in front of me, and my eyes glowed a dark red as I smiled. "My, my, I suspected it was you."

Before I could react, a sudden pain struck through me, making me gasp as my back arched.

I felt a tall, broad spike slice through my heart from behind, tearing through my ribcage and coming out from my front.

I gasped, vision tinting with red as my entire body burned like fire.

I knocked casually on Cammie's bedroom door. "Cammie, are you in there?"

I heard a sigh and a sudden yawn, and Cammie parted the door immediately.

She looked tired as hell but gazed up hazily. "Oh... hey, Alistair. Is everything alright?"

"Yes," I said then, hugging a pillow around myself, "I was on my way to give duchess a new pillow. Hers is a little ruffled and she doesn't look comfortable on it. But I thought I'd stop by here first.

"I was wondering if you could give duchess this in the morning," I said then, handing her a letter. "She is fast asleep right now and I think it would be better."

Cammie just gazed up, taking the letter. "Oh, of course... why?"

But I already walked off.

I felt her staring after me but didn't do anything else to explain.

After stepping through the halls, I ended up at duchess's bedroom, opening the door silently and shutting it behind me.

I then let go of the pillow, lifting her head as she moaned in annoyance, but stuffed it under her.

She just remained asleep, but I knew I possibly woke her up.

I just left the room, knowing there was one last thing I had to do in the kitchen before returning.

8

Hazel
He's Not Dead (Continued)

"Duchess Hazel," Sir Jeffery said, making me gaze up hazily, "what are you doing up at this hour?"

I lightly rubbed my eyes, previously somehow putting on some skirt that I found in my dresser along with my nightshirt.

It took me an hour to button it, though... how did Alistair do these things?

I gazed up then, finding my three servants (excluding Alistair), Madam Savage, and Sir Jeffery surrounding the dining table, staring at a bunch of notes scattered among there.

"You're asking me?" I said then, lightly rubbing my eyes. "What are all of you doing out here this time of night?"

"Oh," Madam Savage said, smiling kindly. "We couldn't sleep. So, we were just going through the mystery upon us."

"Yeah," Cammie said then, "all the suspects are chained up and asleep. I made sure of it. I want to be as of any assistance I can, really."

"I feel the same," Maddox stated.

I then stepped over to the table. "Oh, well... did you find anything?"

They all sighed and shook their heads. "We know not, my lady," Sir Jeffery said. "This is infuriating, indeed."

I wonder what Deneise found then... what did she find that gave away the mastermind's person?

I shook it from my thoughts. "Do any of you know where Alistair is? I felt him leave about five minutes ago, and he woke me up."

I was a little mad at him about it, but never mentioned it.

"And now I'm trying to find him. I need sleeping pills, I swear." I sighed heavily.

They all chuckled in agreement.

"I don't know where Alistair went," Carter said then, scratching the back of his head. "Usually, he cleans the library this time of night, but this is a yacht. There's no library here."

"Laaaaame," Savage said then. "Some of us book nerds need some peace."

I ignored her, though, feeling a little on edge despite my grogginess. "Anyone have ideas of where me might've gone?"

"Knowing, Alistair... caretaker things," Cammie said then. "Cleaning, tidying, fixing your clothes. At this time of night, though... check the kitchen, bedrooms, and maybe the laundry room."

"Thanks..." I said tiredly.

It was weird how she knew these things, but whatever.

"Why don't you stay here for a little bit?" Carter suggested. "I think it better to search for him together with that killer lurking around."

"Yes, I agree," Savage said, smiling over at me. "Don't need someone as precious as you getting killed, that's for sure."

I gave her a tired look. "I'm not sure if I should be pleased or offended."

Cammie laughed quietly. "Duchess, you're very tired, aren't you? Do you want me to escort you to bed? We can look for Alistair while you sleep."

"No," I said then, settling on a chair next to them, "I want to give him a piece of my mind."

"Oh..." Maddox said, inhaling through his teeth, "knowing duchess... that doesn't sound pleasant."

I just smiled weakly.

Ugh... this was taking longer than I thought it would.

After they cleaned up their hellish mess—which took twenty minutes—we searched the entire ship for him.

We checked the laundry room, he wasn't there. We checked the living area, not there.

The billiard room was empty.

The last thing to check before the bedrooms would be the kitchen, so we went there first.

It was very dark in here for this time of night, and I was more awake and aware after all the walking I just did.

I sighed and flicked on the lights, expecting to find nothing.

I froze, body growing cold.

But there wasn't nothing.

"Oh, my God..." Cammie said quietly, covering her mouth.

Alistair lay on the floor of the kitchen, eyes rolled to the top of his head as his breathing and movements were absent.

His irises were small, tiny, almost, and his pupils were miniscule, like tiny little dots in the center of the dulled red.

And there was a large, wooden steak sliced through his chest from in front, penetrating his heart.

I stared for a moment as everyone who followed me gathered at the door.

"Duchess," Cammie said quietly, "duchess, I'm...."

I then stepped in the room, feeling oddly numb. "I don't like these games you're playing with me, Alistair."

He never responded.

"Duchess," Carter said quietly.

"You are to wake up this instant," I said then, voice dark. "Stop it. We both know you're playing dead. This isn't funny."

He still did not respond, remaining weak and motionless from under me.

"Really?" I said then, glaring as my heart cracked and shattered. "Is this what you're going to do? You're to wake up *this instant*! I mean it! WAKE UP, ALISTAIR!"

He still didn't respond.

I then kicked him in the face, making it snap to the side.

"*Duchess*!" Maddox cried.

"I SAID TO WAKE UP!" I yelled then, dropping to his chest to straddle him. I shook him heavily despite the tears burning my eyes. "WAKE UP THIS INSTANT! I MEAN IT! DO YOU HEAR ME? I MEAN IT!"

No, he wasn't dead.

You cannot kill Alistair. He was a demon!

He just remained weak from under me, body limp as I continued shaking him.

I was sick of this GAME!

I then slapped him across the face, making Cammie cry out and hide her face. "WAKE UP, ALISTAIR! STOP THIS GAME THIS INSTANT! WAKE UP, NOW! STOP THIS RIGHT NOW! DO YOU HEAR ME?"

Maddox just came over to me. "Duchess!"

Carter followed behind him, catching me by under my armpits and pulling me off him.

"Let me GO!" I screamed, tears slipping down my cheeks as I kicked. "He's not DEAD! HE'S FAKING! HE'S NOT DEAD! DO YOU HEAR ME? LET ME GO! YOU CANNOT KILL HIM! NO ONE CAN KILL HIM!"

NO ONE COULD KILL ALISTAIR!

HE WAS SWORN TO ME! SWORN TO PROTECT ME!

NO MEASLY HUMAN COULD KILL HIM, EVER!

"Duchess, stop!" Cammie cried then, running over to me. "Stop, please!"

I continued fighting them, my heart cracking more and more.

I shattered then, screaming at the top of my lungs as the cold air devoured me.

Tears slipped down my cheeks, my body growing more and more distant from reality. I was shaking... I was cold... I was... alone.

Maddox and Carter dropped me then, and Cammie rushed over and fell to her knees.

She pulled me into a hug first, and the other two followed suit.

Madam Savage and Jeffery stood at the door, watching me carefully and with a level of sadness and recollection—as if they'd experienced this before and related—but they just stayed in place, unsure of what to do.

I clutched onto Cammie's shirt. "He's not dead! He's not!"

"Duchess..." she said gently.

"HE'S NOT DEAD! HE'S FAKING!"

"Duchess, it's okay," Maddox whispered, holding me tightly. "You'll be okay."

No, I wouldn't.

Without Alistair, I couldn't... without him...

I couldn't live.

"This one could've been anyone," Madam Savage said then, and I was now sitting in a dining room chair numbly, a blanket wrapped around me as Cammie sat at my side.

She gently rubbed my back, making me feel a little better, but not enough.

Never enough.

"Duchess..." Cammie said gently, "would you like me to wash your pillow?"

I gazed over at her in question. "Why?"

"Well... I found a blood stain on the underside, so I was just curious. That's all."

I blinked. "A blood stain?"

She nodded.

I just itched my forehead. "I guess I do have bloody noses at night, don't I?"

"According to the only doctor on this ship," Savage continued, gazing over at the crowd as I listened now. "Madam Beth. She states that Alistair died not even ten minutes before we found him. So that would make only me, Duchess Damonclove, Sir Jeffery, and her three servants innocent. Of course, Madam Beth, Madam Beham, and Lady Jamison were chained in their rooms, but there was no one else to watch them. Everyone else was also in their rooms, alone, despite Duchess Damonclove's wishes to stay together. So basically... *anyone* could be the culprit."

"That makes things easier," Maddox said sarcastically.

I felt my grandmother watch me with dark eyes. I half-expected her to be glaring at me or giving me a stern look of disappointment, but in reality, she looked... depressed. She looked sad for me.

It was a servant who was killed, and she's not scolding me for grieving so much?

I just closed my eyes tightly and gazed up. "It's time we up our game."

Everyone gazed up then, brows drawing together.

"Alistair's death was merely a sign of power," I said then, standing up and pulling off the blanket. "This—alone—makes things harder for me because I'm down two servants now."

And two body-guards.

"Has anyone noticed something, though…?" Madam Claudia said then. "This odd thing keeps popping up in my head. Everyone who's been killed recently… has been somewhat close to Duchess Damonclove… a protector. It seems as if someone's trying to rid of Duchess Hazel's safety net."

"Well, that would explain Scarlet and Alistair's death, but what of Madam Deneise and Sir Denver?"

My lashes lowered.

Sir Denver was more seemed like a scare, and Scarlet was more personal.

Although… Deneise was murdered because she found the truth, and Alistair was murdered to rid of my main bodyguard.

My lashes lowered.

She might not have been wrong.

"But the murders suddenly changed…" Sir Jeffery said then, shaking his head. "The first two looked premediated, used the same weapon, and were aimed directly to the heart. And the murder weapon wasn't found at the scene. Whereas with Deneise, suddenly it was as if the murderer grew impulsive… used a vase as a weapon instead. And Alistair? He was killed with a wooden steak. Doesn't anyone find it odd that the killer is suddenly using tools found at the scene to kill?"

"Yes, that does seem odd," Madam Savage said then. "That's very curious."

"Maybe there are two murders, after all," Sir Jeffery said then.

I sighed and pinched the bridge of my nose, thinking through this strongly.

It was so much harder without Alistair, though. Did I really use him as a crutch that much? Jesus… I was helpless.

But I saw a shadow move to my right, and I glanced over, finding nothing there.

I then looked forward.

"I disagree," I said then, making everyone look over to me in question. "Three of us have been suspects but with some murders that happened, they weren't and no one else was, either. I think it might be possible we have a shadow hiding in the walls."

Everyone looked over to me then, eyes wide.

"A person not in this group?" Jeffery said then. "That seems so obvious! Why didn't I think of that?"

"Who could this person be?" Savage said, shaking her head. "Has anyone seen shadows lurking around anywhere?"

"No, as a matter of fact, I haven't," I said then.

Everyone else shook their heads in response.

"There was this man, though..." Claudia said then, brows drawing together as she recalled the memory, "he was on the ship when we departed. I haven't seen him since."

I gazed up.

She saw him, too?

"He had black hair..." she continued, "wearing an odd trench coat... and had odd eyes."

My lashes lowered immediately, but I remained silent.

Cammie suddenly patted my wrist, and I glanced over at her.

She just slid me a note and glanced down at me. "*Alistair told me to give this to you*," she whispered quietly.

I blinked and gazed down at the note, lightly taking it.

Why would he have done this...?

But—since no one was looking—I opened the note and gazed down at the text:

Hello, my young Duchess.

Yes, I know this may be confusing to you, but I have an explanation.

I think it's safe to assume that someone's planning my demise, and I think it better to be safer than sorry. You are fast asleep right now and I don't want to wake you."

My lashes immediately lowered.

He planned this... he planned his murder.

That is very unusual of him, I must say. Something tells me this isn't over.

He planned this. I knew something was off about this situation.

He knew he was going to die... and he didn't see fit to say goodbye?

I shoved away the pain growing inside and kept reading anyway:

"You asked me who the man in the trench coat was, and if I knew him.

I do know him. You do, too.

I am honestly surprised you didn't recognize him. You need to be more alert, duchess.

Anyway, I will say his name. But my knowledge of him being the murderer remains unknown.

The name of the man in the shadows.

"*Edward*".

My eyes widened immediately, and I clutched the paper tighter.

"You need not to worry, duchess. You have a savior following you.

I promise, you're safe. He will not hurt you.
Ever.

- Alistair."

I stared down at the paper in question, the letter rattling with my tremors.

A savior...?
Who?

Introducing Part 24 – Victim Number Five

Chapter 9

9

Hazel
Victim Number Five

It happened again.

It would've happened again no matter what.

But this time, it was two people... two of my guests murdered at the same time.

I was getting exhausted, honestly.

If Edward was really the culprit, how must I stop him?

I had to figure this out, but all my leads turned into dust.

He was a demon; it wasn't like I could find him. He would remain in the shadows until he wanted me to see him.

Just. Like. Alistair.

But two victims were murdered this time; two of which made me burn with anger and seethe to my heart's content.

They were great people, and they served me great use...

Madam Savage and Sir Jeffery.

Murdered at the same time, during the *day*, nonetheless. We just needed to get back to shore and escape this madness, but we still were twenty-four hours away.

Sir Jeffery...

Murdered at ten o'clock last night with blunt force trauma to the head. Found in the bathroom eight hours later, with a shower pole as the murder weapon.

Madam Savage...

Murdered at ten o'clock last night, as well, although killed by a poisoning.

Cyanide. The first poisoning in this case of murders.

I lowered my lashes as I paced my room, setting my finger on my chin as I thought.

After all these murders, why didn't everyone stay together?

They did mostly, which was why my family wasn't touched. All of the people being killed were my servants and my other guests.

Which was odd, wasn't it? Were they all just this dumb?

Denver was the first, he wouldn't have known.

Scarlet was the second, although we wouldn't have expected a serial murderer.

Deneise was an idiot... she should've never left herself alone that night.

Alistair planned his, though. Which was still odd.

But Savage and Jeffery? They thought they had it under control. They decided to stay together, because safety and numbers was better than the latter. They ended up being killed together.

If Edward was the culprit... he sure had everyone twined around his fingers.

People were smart, they knew how to be safe. But fear? Fear was a dangerous feeling, a horrific emotion. It masked our thoughts on intellect and witnessing the situation. The only ones who knew how to remain calm were the ones who lived.

A shadow moved to my right again, but I ignored it.

That's how life worked, anyway. The smart ones were the ones who lived.

I continued pacing before I stopped, and my lashes lowered.

Like me.

I gazed up to my bedroom door, eyes darkening. "I know you're here, Edward. You've been following me since last night. Show yourself."

There was silence for a moment.

But a low, dark chuckle echoed through the room, sending chills through my spine.

I spun around then, breaths stilling when the lights from the room blew out, and my shadow that casted on the wall grew higher and higher.

It morphed into something horribly menacing, growing darker around the edges.

My hair and dress suddenly blew with a non-existent wind, and I stepped backwards, watching the shadow morph and deform.

"My, my, duchess..." the monster said, making my eyes widen, "how dare you confuse me with that low-life?"

My breaths stilled as my eyes rounded.

I knew that voice.

My shadow suddenly came from the wall, flying outward spinning around me like a hurricane—like shreds of black clothing.

My eye patch immediately came free with the force, flying away like it was trapped in a storm.

My eyes grew in amazement. I could still see.

I kept watching, though, staring as it flew forward and clashed with the air, the others following with it.

Forming a figure.

I continued staring as the silhouette grew higher and clearer.

The moment I saw his black and red tuxedo, my entire being shattered.

I dashed toward Alistair at light speed.

He immediately gasped when I threw my arms around him and held him against me.

My breaths shortened when I buried my face in his chest blazer and fisted his in my hands.

I knew it.

I fucking knew it.

But—even so—he scared me. He scared me shitless.

Alistair just lowered his lips to my head, smiling against me. "Did you really think it would be that easy to rid of me?"

I blinked and pulled away, taking two steps backwards as my cheeks burned a bright red. "I hoped."

He just chuckled, smile widening at my embarrassment. "Duchess, you know you shouldn't underestimate me so."

I just held myself, avoiding eye contact.

He watched me for a moment, but his eyes softened with his smile. "Duchess… were you crying?"

I sniffled and turned away from him. "No. Allergies. You know."

"Aww," he said, chuckling, "that's adorable. You were grieving me."

"Shut up," I snapped, "I wasn't."

"You're a very bad liar," he said, clearly smiling at me. "Especially knowing the last night you thought I was asleep, and you unbuttoned my shirt and snuggled with my chest. Were you really that cold?"

"I don't know what you're talking about," I stated, closing my eyes and tipping my chin up.

I knew what he was talking about. I didn't realize that demons could be so warm, like a campfire! Seriously, I thought they'd be ice cold like vampires or something.

Alistair just stepped around so he could face me, and I gazed up in question. His smile was all fox, menacing. "Mmm..." he said then, lightly tipping my chin up as my eyes widened. "Liar."

He then brought his mouth down on mine, making my eyes bug out when he fisted my hair in his hand and held me in place.

But I couldn't hold back any longer. I swore if I kept fighting his touch I was going to explode or die from a brain hemorrhage.

And... I thought he died. Maybe I could spend a little more time with him...? My life wasn't endless, after all.

I lightly caught the back of *his* head and pulled him closer, making him smile against me.

He clearly knew I gave in, but he said nothing.

I closed my eyes, wanting to drown in this moment.

He tasted like mint, fresh, and earthy. He smelled like sandalwood and freshly carved trees.

How could a demon be so lovely?

I took in every second of this, feeling him catch my bottom lip and let it slip out, and I held back a small moan.

But he finally separated from me, making my lashes part as his face remained inches from mine.

"Why did you do it?" I said gently. "Faking your own death?"

He brushed his fingers through my hair. "Because you told me to fix this. And it would be much easier to catch the killer when they think your main bodyguard is dead."

I gazed up at him then. "Do you know who the killer is?"

He just smiled, eyes glowing dangerously.

"Is it Edward?" I asked him then.

His lashes lowered. "I shall explain when all my preparations are finished, my lady. As of now, there are many problems you are going to face. You must listen to me very carefully, understand?"

"It's me who gives the orders," I said angrily.

He just smiled, lightly tapping my lips with his finger. "Not if your life is in danger."

I blinked at the act and gazed up at him. "Alright, whatever. Out with it, then."

He just closed his eyes with his smile. "Listen very closely, understand?"

Introducing Part 25 – Movement in the Shadows

Chapter 10

10

Hazel
Movement in the Shadows

I swallowed something hard as I stared at the drink settled at the dining table, watching the soft bubbles from the soda fizz and raise to the top.

I narrowed my eyes down at it, watching it suspiciously.

"Duchess Hazel..." that Claudia girl said, voice soft. "Aren't you going to eat your dinner?"

I gazed up then, lips thinning. "I'm not that hungry, actually. I don't know how you *all* are after all that's happened."

Madam Beth set down her chicken leg, gazing up at me in boredom. "At least drink your soda. You don't have to be so wasteful."

"Mom's right," Matilda said then, voice back to its snotty-self. "Eat your food, you selfish brat."

I just closed my eyes and set my napkin aside.

Now that they assumed Alistair was gone, they thought they could treat me like trash again.

A slight smile curled my lips.

Well... they were in for a rude awakening.

I sighed as I set my drink down and stood, brushing the wrinkles off my dress. "Well, I shall head back to my study. I have some work to do."

I then continued forward, glancing over at Matilda as she tore into her dinner and chewed loudly.

Their confidence sank back in despite all of us lying before death's door. How unfortunate.

But—suddenly—Jamison stole my drink from where it stood, immediately gazing up at me. "If you are so wasteful, I'll drink it for you!"

I smiled slightly. "I wouldn't do that if I were you."

"Why not?" Kate said then, eyes narrowing in distaste. "You're not going to drink it, you selfish brat! Is she not allowed to touch your things? Are you possessive over them? Poor thing."

"No, she's right, Jamison," Madam Beth said then, voice soft. "Don't steal someone else's drink, alright?"

I just glanced over at her, watching her from the corner of my eye.

My lashes lowered.

"Why not, mom?" Kate snapped. "Not everything belongs to her, you know."

"That's not my concern," I said then, smile sharpening as I closed my eyes. "I'm just saying don't drink it if you want to live. That soda's laced with cyanide."

All of their faces paled, and they gazed over at me in question.

"How do you know that?" Aunt Beth said then, eyes growing in fear. "Someone's trying to kill you, too?"

"It seems as if you're correct, Madam Beth," I said, looking over at her. "And how I know?" I tapped my forehead. "Intuition."

I then turned and stepped out the door, my dress blowing with the act.

And Alistair warned me of it.

I honestly should've never fallen for "Alistair's death". The mark on my side had been there the whole time. If only I'd looked down and saw it existed, I wouldn't have assumed that he was gone.

As I continued down the hall, a shadow rushed around me.

I stopped and turned to the right, eyes narrowing as a figure leaned against a wall of the hallway, tapping his long, black nails on the whitened paint.

"I was wondering when you'd show yourself," I said then, lashes lowering. "*Augustus.*"

He just giggled and set his head against the wall. "Oh, Little Damonclove. How it's been so long. I longed to see your face since the day I last saw you."

"And I longed to shove a dagger in your throat the moment I realized all of this has been you," I snapped.

"Oh, my," he said then, giggling, "someone's feeling feisty tonight. Aren't you a little on edge?"

"Everyone's being murdered," I answered darkly, "I wonder why."

"Oh, I know nothing of it," he said then, tapping his fingers on the paint again. "I just snuck on the dock to get a little ocean air is all."

"I find that hard to believe," I growled. "You—of all people—don't care about typical lifestyles, Augustus. I swear I will figure out what you're up to and destroy what you're planning."

He just smiled. "What *I'm* planning?"

"The dolls," I stated then, lashes lowering, "those people you murder and model into dolls. It's heartless."

"Oh, my." He lightly touched his chin. "Someone is misinformed."

I stared for a moment, lashes lowering in annoyance. "What?"

"I am not the mastermind," he said, giggling again. "I am simply the underdog."

I narrowed my eyes. "You aren't the father?"

"Ah, no," he said, smile widening, "although that would be nice, wouldn't it?"

"Then what part of this game are you playing at?" I snapped.

"I am merely an underdog," he responded, "as I said. I get the bodies and prepare them. I create the machinery that can turn those ugly humans into gorgeous perfection."

I clenched my fists at my sides, teeth gritting.

But I remained calm.

He makes machinery for me. It makes sense that he would prepare the parts.

I could ask him who the father was, but I knew he wouldn't tell me. Or he would lead me in the wrong direction.

That's what Augustus does.

I just gazed up then, eyes narrowing. "Did you bring any of those... *creatures* with you?"

"No," he said, pouting a little, "sadly. They would make great staff, though, but there a little fidgety with their brains all scrambled. Sadly, I had to leave them home."

I glared. "Pity."

He gazed up then, lips curling again. "I've been watching the game you've been a part of. It's quite fun. I wish I was intertwined with your murders, too. It's quite a mystery to solve, indeed. Let alone that you are the only one who knows Alistair is alive? How interesting. The more the blood splatters, the more the murderer doesn't see what's coming their way."

I just glared sharper. "You're sick."

"I am a fallen angel," he said, lashes lowering over his florescent, green eyes, "I live to see death."

I just clenched my fists tighter.

"You know..." Augustus said, eyes glowing a bright green, "you should watch out. Your little Alistair isn't the only demon roaming around here."

I lowered my lashes. "Edward's here, too?" I scrunched my nose in disgust. "I knew it. I knew he was the one killing all these people."

Augustus just smiled, chuckling darkly. "I never said that, did I?"

Introducing Part 26 – A Second Attempt

C*hapter 11*

11

Hazel
A Second Attempt

I was about to sit down on my bed, but Alistair caught my arm and reeled me forward, making me gasp and stumble when I clashed with his chest.

I gazed up in annoyance, eyes narrowing. "What the hell what that for?"

He remained silent as he stepped over to the mattress and drew back the sheets, and I watched him carefully.

He just picked up a small, thin, shiny object and examined it.

My eyes widened.

A pin? A needle? No... a pin from a sewing set.

Alistair just raised it up and lightly ran his tongue along it.

I stiffened despite the fire rising inside.

He just looked over at me, smiling. "Poisoned. If this pricked you, death would be clear."

I stared for a moment, and he just stepped around me and tossed it into the trash can.

He then stopped next to me. "Come, duchess. Someone's clearly trying to kill you, so I think better if we go to a room where they will not know you will be."

He lightly pulled off his blazer and wrapped it around my shoulders, letting the collar drape over my head to conceal my face.

I gazed up hazily, but he threw me up at an instant, making me yelp as my legs flew upward at the act. But I suddenly landed in his arms, bouncing slightly before I settled down.

"Come now," he said, eyes softening. "We must hurry."

I set my head on his shoulder, wrapping my arms around his neck to keep myself steady.

And maybe seeking a little comfort... I wouldn't ever admit that, though.

He then carried me out of the room, smiling slyly as if he could tell I was giving in.

"My, my, is that little Hazel Damonclove, I see?" a dark voice said as Alistair carried me down the hall.

Alistair slowed to a stop as I gazed over hazily, lashes lowering when I saw Edward standing against a wall, hands in his pockets.

Ugh... he was blocking the way. This hall was too thin for all of us to fit through.

Alistair was trying to take the secret route through a passageway. Why did they make these so small?

"Excuse me, but I must go down that way. If you don't mind moving, that would be much appreciated, indeed," Alistair said too kindly.

Edward just smiled as he gazed down at me. "Don't you think you're getting a little too attached to him? He's the root cause of your demise, isn't he?"

"Your manipulation tactics don't work on me," I said then, lashes lowering. "Don't try it. I'm not signing with you, period. Especially knowing that you're a murderer. Serial, if that, and killed all these people just out of fun."

Edward smiled a little, chuckling as he closed his eyes. "You must think highly of me, indeed. I am only a sightseer; I promise you that."

I gritted my teeth, hearing them crack at the motion. "Bullshit."

He gazed up then. "Believe what you want. This isn't my problem, after all."

"Stop your testing," I snapped then, glaring sharply. "I'm not signing with a lowly demon such as yourself. I have *standards*."

Edward smiled, red eyes glowing dangerously. "Oh, so confident. That's what I love about you. Your blood was the appetizer, now I want the full meal."

Alistair just smiled, eyes glowing in response. "You heard her. Now move out of the way."

Edward just closed his eyes and smiled, stepping aside as Alistair moved past him, carrying me down the hall.

A minute later, we entered an empty bedroom, and Alistair kicked the door closed behind him and carried me over to another mattress.

He laid me down onto it, and I grumbled in annoyance.

"This bed isn't comfy," I complained.

He just smiled. "You're going to have to deal, duchess. This is the only room where the killer won't suspect us."

I closed my eyes tightly.

Sir Denver's room.

I blinked hazily as Alistair readied me for bed, changing my clothes to my night outfit before pulling the sheets over me.

I gazed up at him when he set my eye patch on the nightstand. "Why do you have a change of clothes for me in this bedroom?"

He smiled. "I must always be prepared."

My lashes lowered then, and I pulled the covers higher over myself. "You know who the killer is, don't you?"

He closed his eyes, smile softening. "Yes, and they are going to show themselves tomorrow. Ten minutes before we reach the shore."

"You know this for sure?" I said, blinking.

He gazed down at me. "I cannot lie, duchess."

"But you can be wrong," I stated.

He chuckled. "Since when have I been wrong?"

I was silent for a moment, but I settled into myself. "Rarely."

He gazed down then, watching me carefully.

I stared back up, feeling my eyes glisten with his reflection.

He broke the silence then. "You're not tired, are you?"

I shook my head.

"Even after your midnight milk?" he said then.

I shook my head. "Wide awake."

He just sighed, although the smile was still there. "Duchess, you're going to be the death of me."

"You cannot die," I stated then.

He looked down at me then. "You're right, I cannot."

I just watched him.

But he smiled, leaning down onto the bed as my eyes widened.

His face was inches from mine then, making my breath shutter.

I watched his pupils slit slightly, and my eyes rounded.

"I can help you sleep," he said, the red in his iris glowing dangerously with his fox smile. "I am a demon, after all."

My breath shuttered, and I stared at him.

I caught the hint but didn't move.

"Aren't you going to say no?" he said then, sliding his hand under the covers.

My cheeks burned a bright red, but I said nothing.

His lashes lowered over red eyes, and he pulled the covers down.

I stared as he caught under my shirt and lifted it, exposing my chest as I closed my eyes tightly.

He saw them every day, he bathed them every day, and he clothed them every day.

How could he hold himself back for so long?

Alistair just ran his thumb along a soft bud, making me whimper. "You know..." he said, voice low and smokey, "every time I had sex with someone, I did it for Agnes. To get information out of them."

I parted my eyes, half-annoyed that he was ruining the moment.

"I am a demon after all," he said then, continuing to run his thumb along it again. "But with you, duchess, I do it because I want to. Not that I didn't want to with those women, but these are different circumstances, don't you think?"

I closed my eyes tightly. "You're turning me off."

"Pity," he said then, smiling, "I was trying to be touching."

"You're bad at it."

He just chuckled and gazed up at me. "Your face is redder than a tomato."

I just caught a pillow and covered my mouth and cheeks, hiding it from him.

"No, don't do that," he said then, pulling the pillow away. "Don't hide this side of you from me."

My face burned brighter at his words, but he just smiled and dipped down.

His tongue glided over a sensitive nipple then, covering it entirely as a hot shiver ran through me, making me arch my back.

Somehow, I felt myself grow redder.

He pulled away slightly and brushed my hair away from my face, making me breathe uneasily when he leaned down to set his lips on mine.

I closed my eyes tightly, raising a hand to catch onto his hair.

He smiled against me and caught my wrist, lowering the same hand to his shoulder.

I fisted the fabric, sweat sliding down my temples as my mouth grew watery with arousal.

He pulled away, chuckling lowly. "Duchess, you're always such a spit fire. Why aren't you resisting me?"

I closed my eyes tightly, arching my back and kicking out my legs. "Don't tease me, Alistair!"

"Shhh," he said then, pressing a finger to my lips, "quiet. We don't want the murderer to know we're here, remember?"

I gazed up at his face—right in front of mine—finding a small amount of his teeth showing through his smile… and the red, the red in his eyes glowed oh, so brightly, threateningly.

I let out a breath and nodded, and he just set his forehead on mine, sliding his hand down… and down… under me, into me.

I squeezed my eyes shut tightly, wincing at the small burn, but he kept it minimal.

"Breathe, duchess," he instructed. "You're holding it."

I let out a breath and shook my head, clutching onto his shirt tighter when he started pumping them in and out.

A small whimper escaped my lips, followed by a low moan.

He just set his lips on mine, concealing any further cries.

When he pulled away, he just cooed, "Shhhhhh…."

I tried to breathe, but it was so hard. I just gazed up at him, finding his smile still there.

"Duchess," he said, "you're a virgin, aren't you?"

I nodded once, trying to breathe through this.

"Why are you allowing me this, my lady?" he pressed again. "Do you seriously want a demon to be your first? And your last."

I just gave him a dark smile then. "What, so you want me to go do it with someone else first?"

Alistair's pupils slit. "Never. I'll kill them."

"Then don't suggest it," I said, laughing silently. "Because… because…."

I winced, breaths straining as my back arched.

I squeezed my eyes shut tightly, feeling something inside build higher, and higher...

It released then, and Alistair covered my mouth when I let out a soft cry, body rattling from under him.

Why did this feel so good? What just happened?

It was like my entire soul was filled with warmth, a gorgeous amount of heat and pleasure shivering through me. It was... glorious... it was... heaven-like.

But half-a-minute later, I settled from under him, breathing shakily.

I was suddenly so tired, my body growing distant and numb. I'd never felt so exhausted before.

Was all my previous acts and refusal to sleep catching up with me?

Alistair just pulled his hand away, watching me gently as I gazed up at him.

He just pulled off his glove—the one that he soiled—and he tossed it away to an unknown location.

I didn't care about that anyway.

He pulled off his second glove to make it even.

I breathed softly, gazing up when he kicked off his shoes and settled into the bed next to me.

One second, he was getting under the covers, and the next I was dragged against him, head on his chest and legs splayed across the bed.

I pulled my arms up to catch onto his shirt and snuggled my face into his neck.

Alistair just ran his fingers through my hair, letting me slowly drift. "Go to sleep. We have a big day tomorrow, duchess."

My cheeks burned a bright red, and I closed my eyes tightly.

I gave in.

Shit. I gave in.

I couldn't stop myself now. It wasn't a temptation anymore.

No. Now it's a craving.

Introducing Part 27 – Knowing the Culprit

Chapter 12

12

Hazel
Knowing the Culprit

I kept my eyes closed, head resting on Alistair's chest as he mindlessly stroked my back.

I didn't know if he could tell I was awake or not, but... I was for a while now.

It was early morning, maybe six or seven o'clock. Not my wake-up time, and I was secretly glad it wasn't because I was very comfortable.

I might've been a self-centered brat, but some things I couldn't resist.

I hated to admit that, though.

Alistair was lying on the right side of the bed, left hand under his head as the other one wrapped around my form and rubbed my back.

I could tell he was relaxed and alert at the same time. He just had that stance right now.

I could also tell he was staring at the ceiling, thinking. He was always thinking. *I* was always thinking.

He was going through every possible outcome today, I could tell.

Alistair taught me how to play chess; the number one tool is strategy. Assessing the situation before going in full force. Alistair could assess a situation in a matter of seconds. He had the sight and intellect of a computer, but it was due to him being a demon.

I, on the other hand, was completely human. A human mind, a human body, a human lifespan.

Although, I did have an odd sect of intelligence for a typical eighteen-year-old, everything I knew was taught by Alistair. He gave me schooling lessons, strategic lessons. He taught me nursing material, which gave to my medical knowledge.

He taught me everything I knew.

In reality he already knew what I needed to do to survive in this family... because of Agnes, and he taught me skills that I needed to solve crimes.

So, I was safer...

If he was in it entirely for my life, like he was with Agnes, he sure went out of his way for these things.

Didn't Agnes find that odd, though...? Or did she just not want to accept it?

I shuffled more into Alistair.

You should be asking that question to yourself, Hazel. You are Agnes, and you've been thinking the same things.

I just kept myself relaxed into Alistair, breathing gently.

But—after a moment—I turned further into him, burying my face in his shoulder. "Alistair...."

"Yes, duchess?" His voice was gentle, quiet.

"I'm cold," I said then.

He immediately shuffled against me and pulled the covers up to my nose, tucking them under me so my body heat would catch better.

"Warm enough?" he said then.

I nodded, relaxing back into him again.

He kept rubbing my back.

"I'm dying of curiosity," I said then, gazing up. "Who is it?"

Alistair just smiled. "Haven't you already figured it out?"

I stared back down at his chest, but a low, sly smile spread across my face.

"I thought so," he said then, sighing, "you're very clever, duchess. No one seems to understand that. I'm sure you've figured out everything else, too, haven't you?"

I just closed my eyes and relaxed into his chest, smile still there. "Tell me the plan."

"Thank you all for gathering here today," I said, closing my eyes kindly as we sat at the breakfast table. "It is much appreciated."

Matilda just scoffed, tearing into her meal and chewing loudly. "Why else would we be here? It's food time anyway."

I didn't dare touch my meal, though. Alistair never said anything about it being poisoned, but I wasn't willing to risk it.

"What did you call us out here for, my lovely granddaughter?" Madam Beham said then, smiling slightly. "Is there news you wanted to tell us?"

I glanced over at her. "As a matter of fact, there is."

"Are we close to shore yet?" Kate said then, glaring. "I'm done with this place."

I just gazed up. "We are about five hours from shore, I'm afraid."

She just glared and continued chewing into her food.

"Well, I have some news," I said then, sighing as they all gazed up at me. "About the murders."

"Are you next?" Jamison said then, laughing. "It's about time."

"Yes, as a matter of fact, there have been at least two attempts of murdering me," I stated honestly. "And it takes much effort for me to realize that. It's very unsettling, honestly."

"I hope they succeed," Jamison said then. "You're a spoiled brat."

I just gazed over at her. "I would be careful of how you speak to me, you brainless child."

She threw her head up. "*Excuse me*? I am two years older than you! And why should I be careful?! Your little *caretaker* is no longer around to protect your sorry ass."

I smiled then. "Did you really think he was my only protection?" I closed my eyes sweetly. "Maddox."

He immediately stepped out from the wall and cocked two guns, aiming it at them.

Jamison screamed, throwing herself off the chair and hiding behind it.

Matilda and Kate just shrank back, eyes growing in fear.

"WHAT IS HAPPENING?!" Madam Claudia screamed, scrambling backwards until she met the wall.

"It's alright madam," I said then, gazing up at her. "He will not aim at you, just these children."

All of my family members breathed shallowly, eyes trained on guns aimed at them.

"Now," I said, "Maddox has very good aim. He can shoot all of you in two seconds with a bullet for each person. What is your body count again?"

"Fifty in thirty seconds," he said then.

All of their eyes grew in fear.

"Don't mess with me, children," I said then, lashes lowering. "I have many tricks up my sleeve."

Madam Beth just breathed uneasily as her husband shrank back like his children.

Madam Beham, on the other hand, looked a little relieved. "Back to your old self, I see. Now... the news, Hazel?"

I glanced over at her. "Oh, yes. I found the murderer."

They all gazed up then, eyes widening.

"You did?" Matilda said.

"How?" Madam Beth said.

"Who?" Curtis retorted.

I just gazed up. "The evidence points to four people, but the murderer must only be one."

"You mean..." Claudia said then, sweat sliding down her temples, "there's one murderer? Not two? How is that possible?"

"There must be another person on this boat then!" Matilda said. "That's the only explanation!"

I just smiled, setting my cheek in my hand. "Let's go through all evidence, shall we? First victim, Sir Denver. Stabbed through the heart with a blade. Second victim, Scarlet Manslaughter, stabbed through the heart with the same blade." I gazed up. "Then it changed, third victim, Madam Deneise, hit over the head with a vase and stabbed through the eye with a glass shard. Messy scene, not well planned. Fourth victim," my lashes lowered as my smile fell, "Alistair. Stabbed through the heart with a table leg. Last two victims, Sir Jeffery and Madam Savage. Both murdered differently but at the same time, hit over the head with a shower pole, and poisoned with cyanide."

I gazed up then, the smile forming on my lips. "The first murder, however, pointed directly toward Madam Beham. Which is odd, don't you think? If mama wanted to kill someone, she'd make sure that she wouldn't be caught."

All of them gazed over at her in horror.

"Second victim," I said then, smiling sweetly, "same outcome. But Madam Beham was innocent, and the culprits pointed to Jamison and Aunt Beth."

"So how the hell is there only one murderer?" Curtis questioned.

I pointed up a finger. "Ah, ah. Let me finish." I gazed up. "Didn't you notice that the first two murders were premeditated and planned well? They had the same weapon, same outcome, same timeframe. And centered toward one or two culprits. Whereas the other murders were messy, in the spur of the moment, the murder weapons used were grabbed from the scene it took place in. Let alone the most confusing thing... they pointed to multiple culprits."

All of their brows drew together.

"There is one murderer," I said then, lashes lowering. "And it's Aunt Beth."

Beth immediately stiffened, cheeks burning a bright red. "Excuse me? How could it have been me?! That makes no sense!"

"Yeah, the first murder she had an alibi!" Jamison said then, although I could see her shaking a bit. "You can confirm!"

"Oh, I can," I said then, smiling sweetly. "But it was she who murdered Sir Denver, and the others."

"What evidence do you have?!" Beth yelled.

"The scene of the crime," I said, gazing up. "You are a doctor, correct? You determined the cause of his death was a stab wound to the heart."

"It was!" she yelled then. "Did you not see the blood?!"

"Ah, yes, indeed," I gazed up, "the blood was fake."

Her face immediately paled.

"I recalled Alistair saying something at the scene of the crime," I said then, thinking it over sarcastically. "He said it smelled like almonds. Now, it was a very odd thing to say at that point in time. Very random. But then it got me thinking… what smells like almonds?" I then gazed up. "Cyanide smells like almonds."

She shrank back in her seat then, seething. "How could it have been me? Everyone saw me! Everyone saw what I was doing that night!"

"Ah, yes, but… what if Sir Denver drank it himself?" I said then.

They all gazed up in question.

"I read through Sir Denver's records. You paid for some of his medical bills, and he owed you a favor in return. Now… from Sir Denver's personality, I promise you that no one in the world can withstand him, so the remorse in the murder was lessened… especially by you.

"This is what you did," I said kindly, "you asked him to fake his death."

Everyone's eyes widened.

"You gave him the cyanide and said it would make him sleep, and then when he woke up, he'd be as good as new. So, he poured the fake blood on himself and drank the cyanide. Died shortly after in the hallway, where you told him to go. Before he could scream because everything went wrong, he was dead. And because you're a doctor and no one else is, you knew you'd be assessing the body thoroughly because others cannot stomach it and ruled it a stabbing."

"How the *hell* can you prove me wrong, then?" Beth snapped. "No one else assessed it!"

I laughed then, tipping my head back, but I immediately stared forward. "Did you seriously think that my servants can't stomach an autopsy?"

Her eyes widened then.

"You're smart," I said, lashes lowering. "I'm smarter."

"How can you explain the other deaths, though?" Jamison questioned, voice shaking.

I sighed. "Scarlet's death was the only one who pointed directly to Madam Beth, but... that was purposeful." I looked up with a smile. "That look on your face when you saw she was killed was priceless, I think Alistair did a pretty good job setting it up."

Madam Beth's eyes widened. "What?"

I knocked on the table. "Scarlet. Come out."

A door to our right opened, and a small, thin figure stepped out.

Scarlet, the girl with blonde hair and emerald-green eyes. She closed the door behind her and moved to stand with Maddox.

"What...?" Beth said then, brows drawing together. "*What...?*"

"Alistair planned her death," I stated, smiling. "After Denver died, I asked him to fix this, he did. He made you look the murderer because you are."

Her eyes blazed in anger then. "You... insolent child."

"That's why when Scarlet died, it didn't affect Hazel that much," Kate realized. "Hazel knew it was fake the whole time."

I smiled sweetly. "Indeed, I did. Scarlet did quite a performance, too. With her previous job, it required her to control her breathing. So, she slowed it enough, so her chest didn't rise and fall. She did the same as Denver and poured fake blood on her chest."

"Mom didn't look at her body..." Matilda realized quietly. "When she asked to assess the body, Alistair said he already did and determined it a stabbing. The same as the first."

"What of the other murders then?" Beth retorted, face red in anger. "They were all different."

"Because Alistair scared you," I stated darkly. "He caught you red-handed. And he framed her murder to you, just to see how you'd react. When a murder feels they've been caught, they grow messy, less planned. Try to cover their tracks without thinking of the other prints they'd leave around."

Beth just shook her head, glaring. "How the hell could I have killed that *Deneise* girl when I was locked in that room with *mother and Jamison*?"

I gazed up, laughing softly. "Seriously, are you going to say *locked up*?"

Her brows drew together then.

"Cammie was watching you, indeed," I said then, nodding. "But... here's the thing about leaving prints... when I was outside Deneise's room, I found this on the hallway floor."

I raised a thin, yellow-like yarn that had been cut short. "Yarn sticks to clothes very thoroughly.

"So?" she said then.

"A decoy," I stated, setting the yarn aside. "Of you."

Her teeth clenched. "You have no proof."

My lashes lowered, and I waved my hand to the side.

Cammie stepped out from the wall and opened a closet door, finally tearing out a doll-like figure that replicated Madam Beth.

Everyone gasped, shrinking back in their seats.

"Looks like you," I said then, smiling. "Typical doll-trick. You set the doll on a couch, facing the TV. Then—when Cammie's distracted—you run out of the room, kill Deneise, and then come back. Everyone assumed the doll was still you. It's a very risky trick, but you were not caught." I raised the yarn again. "If you didn't leave this."

Her lips drew back in anger. "And what of Alistair?!"

"Alistair, Savage, and Jeffery's murders could've been anyone," I stated, lashes lowering. "They were done at the dead of night, while people were asleep. You have no alibi for them, I can assure you."

She just clenched her teeth, snarling at me. "You are jumping through hoops here, girl."

"You overcomplicated things for something so simple," I stated, ignoring her comment. "None of the others had to die."

She just shook her head. "My motive? What is my motive?"

I set the yarn aside again. "Me."

"What?" everyone said at once.

"You were planning on killing me," I stated then, voice dark. "I was your main target, wasn't I? Your original plan was to frame Denver's death on someone else and then kill me. You wouldn't be caught then, would you? But this is modern days, Madam Beth. You will be caught eventually."

"What is she going on about?" Beth said then. "Are you *that* self-centered? Everything is about you?"

"Ah, in fact, I am not," I said then, gazing up. "Because you had a motive for killing everyone that died. Whereas others had not."

Her lashes lowered then.

"Denver was the key to pointing the view at Madam Beham," I stated. "Deneise found the truth, so she had to go. Alistair was to get my bodyguard out of the way, same with the last two. Savage and Jeffery had been switching positions and standing outside my door at night when my servants were not. You were planning on poisoning my drink, but they were in the dining room, so you ended up killing them first and then poisoning the drink. But... in the end... I knew the soda was poisoned. My point was proved correct when one of your daughters tried to drink it and you told them not to because 'it's cruel to steal drink from others.' With how much you resent me, I was bound to become suspicious."

She just made an impatient sound. "Are you pulling this all out of your ass right now?"

"Why else would your children and husband be untouched? Why else would you go through no precautions to protect your children when there was a murder on the loose? Why else would Madam Beham be alive...? She is your escape route, after all, isn't she? She was the one to be framed."

"This makes sense, but her motive is all messed up," Claudia said then, brows drawing together. "Why kill you, Hazel?"

"Madam Beth has been craving to be the Damonclove duchess her entire life," I stated then, gazing over at her to find her fuming. "She wanted to be the head of the family, but my father was chosen. When my parents died, she wanted to be it again, but then... I was chosen. A child compared to her. That's why she bullied me all these years; jealously. Her children, too, were jealous. They weren't rich enough to get servants, get any car they wanted, have an ice rink in their basement. I took that away from them. If I died, then she'd be next in line, wouldn't she?"

Beth remained silent, eyes narrowing at me.

Matilda piped up, "Then how can you prove she was the one who attempted to poison your drink?"

"Can you prove against it?" I said then, gazing over at her. "The drink could've been poisoned any time from four in the evening to six in the evening. Anyone was a suspect, once again. I was the only one with that flavor of soda. The whole bottle was poisoned, clearly. Especially knowing it was disposed of right after it was poured for me."

"Why frame her mother?" Claudia said then. "She could've framed you, right? Because you were her last and final victim?

I gazed over. "Good question." I smiled then. "None of the victims could be suspects. It would mess up the entire plan. It would gain suspicion, which was a risk she did not want. And... why my grandmother? It's because Madam Beham was the one who chose my father, and then me. She's mad and feels betrayed. She's not willing to kill her own *mother*, but framing her and sending her to jail? My, my... that would be perfect revenge, indeed. Let alone that Madam Beth's been in town with my grandmother for quite some time. She found out that my grandmother goes to bed early without telling anyone. It was the perfect time to commit the crime, as well, knowing that everyone else would be together in different rooms. Including herself."

She broke then, slamming her hands down on the table. "You little brat! You had it coming!"

I smiled then, chuckling.

Aggravate the perpetrator enough, they will crack and snap, revealing that they committed the crime. Especially knowing that Madam Beth is hot-headed.

"You had *everything* coming!" she snapped, standing quickly. "You should've been gone WHEN YOUR PARENTS DIED! WHY DID IT HAVE TO BE YOU WHO SURVIVED, HUH? WHY?"

I just lowered my lashes, smiling slightly.

"You took EVERYTHING from me!" she yelled, face growing enraged. "My money! My fame! My BUISSNESSES! They were all supposed to be MINE BUT *YOU* TOOK IT!"

She then pulled a knife from her napkin, making her children squeal and fall off their chairs to hiding. "YOU DESERVE TO DIE!"

Maddox raised his gun, but I put out a hand, making him stop.

She then started toward me, but I remained calm.

I gazed up at her then. "Don't do it. I'm warning you."

"Mom!" Matilda cried. "Mom, stop, please!"

"Mom, please, for the love of god!" Kate screamed.

Claudia said nothing, just remained in the corner, face hidden in shadows.

Beth just struck off the ground and came straight toward me, screaming when she caught the knife with both hands and shoved it down onto me.

It was getting closer… and closer.

Inches…

Centimeters…

Millimeters…

But her arm was caught, and she froze, breaths straining.

Her clothes settled around her, flowing down at the stop of movement, and her eyes widened in horror, the light in them dissipating.

I gazed up in boredom.

"I'm sorry, Madam Beth," Alistair said, "but I cannot allow you to hurt my duchess."

She gazed up then, eyes widening in horror. "H… how? HOW?"

His lips curled into a smile, showing a little bit of his teeth. "You seriously thought you killed me? My, duchess was right. When you get impulsive, you do not think of the little things, do you? Like the fact that…" he tipped his head to the side, "I was a demon?"

Her eyes grew in shock.

He just flicked his wrist, and she went flying, screaming and covering her face with her arms as she slid down the table.

Plates fell around at her movement, clashing with the floor and covering it in sharpened ceramic.

But she flew off the table and clashed with the wall, back cracking at the act.

I set my cheek in my hand, feeling Alistair's demonic presence swarm around me like a black fire.

"Alistair's not dead...?" Matilda said then, eyes widening.

"Oh, God..." Kate whispered.

Jamison watched him, horror-struck.

But Claudia...? Still in the corner, hiding her face.

Scarlet and Maddox just closed their eyes and bowed, stepping backward to the wall where Carter and Cammie stood. They were clearly keeping a distance, letting Alistair take care of the rest.

And he did.

Alistair's smile sharpened as the candles around us blew out, and everyone let out scattered cries and whimpers of fear.

The lights flickered and burst, shattering in a matter of seconds.

Everyone screamed, all except for me, Beham, and my servants.

My lashes lowered when the shards of glass and plastic rained around us, although they never touched my skin.

The room grew dark despite the sunlight bleeding through the parted curtains, black swarming around us as a sudden wind blew my hair to the side.

My entire family screamed and huddled in a corner, attempting to shield each other from what was to come.

Madam Beham just remained in her seat, sipping her chai casually.

Alistair's low chuckle echoed through the room, bursting from nonexistent speakers. "Did you really think? That you can attempt to kill me, and then harm my duchess?

And get away with it?"

They covered their heads when the wind grew harder.

Madam Beth just screamed and shot up, dashing straight over to the doors to the ship.

But Alistair was there in seconds, making her scramble to a stop.

His smile was dark, his teeth sharpening to spikes as his demonic eyes glowed through his shadow. "Where are you going to go? Swim to shore? The ocean will kill you, you know. Depressing. Is that really how you wanted to go?"

She took steps backward, and he followed with her, walking forward at the same pace.

Her eyes grew in fear as he towered over her, but his smile sharpened.

"Duchess," he said, "may I?"

They all looked to me in horror, Madam Beham still sipping her chai.

I gazed up then, lips curling into a smirk as I pulled the string of my eye patch, letting it fall.

The mark in my right eye glowing a bright yellow as my lashes lowered.

"Hazel, please, don't!" Matilda cried, breath shaking. "We're your family!"

I ignored her though, tipping my head to the side. "Don't worry. I'll make a nice memorial for you." I gazed up then. "Alistair, kill them."

The crescent scar on my side burst with light, beaming through my dress... and the mark in my eye followed, the X glowing a bright yellow.

Alistair's smile widened as he lowered his head, chuckling.

"**I would love to, duchess**."

"Alistair, are you almost done?" I said as he lightly picked up the last article of clothing from his victims.

"Indeed, this is the last of it," he said then, lightly tossing it in the air and hovering his hand up.

The clothing caught fire, disintegrating in seconds, not even leaving ash behind.

He then lowered his hand, dusting them off before stepping over to me.

"Your gloves are still off," I stated then.

"I know, duchess," he said gently. "I told you; I soiled them."

I felt my cheeks burn, and I just sipped my chai to hide it.

"So," I said then, lowering my chai as Madam Beham looked toward the corner casually, "are you going to stand there the whole time? Or are you going to move?"

Madam Claudia remained in the corner; face still hidden in the shadows.

"You've been standing there for twenty minutes now," I said then, Alistair smiling as he lightly poured more chai into my cup. "You are very good at pretending, aren't you? Really, you'd be a good actress." I smiled up. "Augustus, right?"

Claudia immediately looked up, eyes darkening immediately at my stare.

She just smiled and set a hand against her face.

She then tipped her head back, tearing off her mask immediately and ripping her fake face to shreds.

"My, my," Alistair said then, "duchess, you were right. He was hiding among the guests."

"I'm always right, Alistair," I stated honestly.

Augustus just gazed up, setting his finger against his chin as he winked at me. "My lady, how could you tell?"

"Claudia kept switching personalities," I said then, sighing as I set my cheek in my hand. "And Edward wasn't acting like himself, either."

Augustus just smiled. "You knew he was a fake, too?"

"There were twenty people entering the ship immediately when it was docked," I said then, lashes lowering. "And there were twenty people in the dining room. Four were actually murdered and confirmed to be dead, two were faked and roaming around, leaving only my family members, my servants... and... *you* were the only guest left. I just connected the pieces. Having Edward roaming around the ship without adding count to the guests was simple. And also," I gestured to Alistair, "he can sense things. He sensed no demons, just a fallen."

Augustus just smiled. "How very bright you are."

I sipped my chai. "What do you want?"

"Oh, I was looking through what would be happening today, and I saw a bunch of murders happening on this ship! And then I saw you centered around it. I just couldn't resist. I am an immortal man; I deserve some entertainment every once and a while. And boy, oh, boy, should I do this more often."

I just gave him a bored look. "What happened to the real Claudia?"

"Oh, don't worry about her," he shook his hand, "she's asleep in her bed. She never even got the invitation, she's quite alright."

"And the father?" I continued. "He's not mad that you're missing?"

Augustus scoffed. "I'm his buyer, he doesn't care."

Alistair poured more chai into my cup again, remaining silent, but amused.

I drank from it, setting it down.

"Well," Augustus said then, winking at me, "I must go now. It was a pleasure witnessing this play with you, my lady. But there are other matters to attend to." He then danced around a bit. "*Toodles*!"

And he hopped backwards like some acrobat, out the window and into the sea.

"He's going to swim to shore?" I said, half-annoyed.

"Well, we're only ten minutes out now, my lady," Alistair said.

I sighed then. "Good. There's some shopping I need to do."

I then looked over at my grandmother. "You've been very quiet, Madam Beham. Why is that?"

She just smiled and set her chai aside. "There's a reason why I chose you as heir, Hazel. A very good reason, indeed. You don't let your personal matters get in the way of your physical preparations of war." She gazed up. "I assessed every situation and your reactions. You knew that the first murder was from Denver himself immediately. That's why you were so calm and unafraid of me. You also helped Alistair plan Scarlet's show, didn't you?"

My lashes lowered.

"Deneise's is what really took you off guard," Madam Beham said then. "Because it wasn't planned. And you genuinely thought Alistair died, didn't you?"

I was silent.

"Now... my real question." She shuffled in her seat. "Why did you invite us on this ship? You knew she was planning this, didn't you?"

I sighed. "I did, indeed."

"Why didn't you stop her?" Madam Beham said then.

"I chose my crowd for a reason," I stated, sipping my chai again.

She stared for a moment, before smiling. "You wanted them to die, didn't you?"

I gazed over at her, smiling slightly. "You are very insightful. I think that's where I get it from." I then sighed and set my head against the chair. "Alas, yes, I wanted them to die... most of them. Alistair explained to me before my invitations were sent, that Madam Beth was planning my demise. So, I sought fit to use her as a pawn."

Cammie just blinked. "Wow, duchess, really? You planned all this?"

I nodded. "In all honesty, Deneise was the only one I didn't want to die. She was supposed to be my witness. I actually thought Denver was her only victim, which was why Scarlet's faked death was premeditated beforehand. But she freaked out and killed Deneise, the only one I was weary about ridding of." I gazed up. "Everyone else, I cared less of.

"Denver rolled in drugs and weapons illegally through the states for money. Sir Jeffery committed multiple acts of felonies and harassed teenage girls—to put it lightly. And Madam Savage murdered her boss to get in her job place. Beth murdered Jeffery and Savage because she thought they were my bodyguards, in reality, they were planning my demise, as well."

"My, everyone's plotting, aren't they?" Beham just smiled, drinking her chai again. "And was Claudia supposed to die, too?"

I nodded. "Yes, she was another one of my targets, yes. She's part of a trafficking ring, who isn't?" I rolled my eyes. "But I will get to her later."

Alistair just adjusted my tie in place and then poured me the last of the chai.

"You were planning to kill your aunt and your cousins the whole time," Beham said then. "Which was why you invited them."

I gazed up, smile sharpening. "She thought I was doing it out of kindness and thought she premeditated everything. She was planning to kill me, and I had the right to protect myself. Let alone all the bullying that my cousins displayed on me. They were kind and sappy, but once Alistair 'died' they switched back to normal. Proved me right, they never changed. They were just afraid of him." I sighed. "Madam Beth might be smart," I sipped my chai, "I'm smarter."

Beham just closed her eyes and smiled. "Indeed, you are. Your intellect scares me just a bit."

"A very clever girl," Alistair added, bowing, "duchess."

Introducing Part 28 – Done with Waiting

Chapter 13

13

Hazel
Done with Waiting

"Are you all packed, my lady?" Alistair said then, standing next to me.

His lips immediately parted when he gazed down at what I was holding.

The pillow he left me the night he died, I was holding it, staring down at it. "It was a clue, wasn't it?" I said then, lashes lowering as I ran my finger along the bloodstain. "That you were still alive?"

He stared down at it for a moment but smiled. "Indeed, it was."

"You gave the letter to Cammie after your 'death,'" I said then. "You gave me this pillow after you were stabbed, as well. This blood... is yours."

His smile softened. "Indeed, duchess, it is."

I just set the pillow down onto the bed and gazed up at him. "Do not do that again, understand?"

"Do what again?" he said then.

My anger faltered then, and I shrank back into myself while looking away. "Don't... scare me like that. I actually thought you were gone."

He just watched me.

I shoved my bag against his chest. "I'm ready. Let's go."

He lightly took the bag from me and smiled, but I just walked past him and made my way out the door.

But my wrist was caught, and I was shoved back into the room.

I yelped and stumbled backward, colliding with the mattress seconds later.

When I got up, Alistair just closed the door, setting my back down beside it.

"Excuse me?" I said then, glaring. "Since when can you handle your duchess like that?"

"We can spare a couple minutes. The ship hasn't docked yet." He just gazed up at me with a sinister smile, and my face paled a little.

Uh, oh.

He stepped back over to the bed, and I scrambled further onto it.

"You don't want to soil your gloves again," I stated, shrinking away.

He gazed down at his freshly cleaned gloves and blinked. "Oh, you are right, once again, duchess. I guess it can't be helped." He lightly bit the finger of his right glove and pulled it off, doing the same with his second.

My face paled even more.

Crap. I thought that would've worked.

"I'm on my period!" I said then.

He just chuckled. "No, you're not. Don't lie."

I remained silent again.

Right... he helped me change so he would've known. Uh... crap.

"My stomach's upset," I argued then. "Nasty diarrhea."

His smile widened. "You're a bad liar, you know."

I felt my cheeks burn a bright red.

Alistair just smiled down at me. "If you don't want me to do this, then why don't you tell me to back away?"

I looked away then, face burning a bright red.

He knelt beside the bed. "Is duchess scared?"

"Shut up," I said then, shooting him a look. "Do not accuse me of such idiotic emotions."

His eyes glowed dangerously. "Duchess, can I be frank with you?"

I looked down at him in suspicion.

"If I might be honest, I have been very patient with you," Alistair said then, lashes lowering over red eyes. "All these years, I have. Our contract has changed, I am still patient, and now... I'm done with waiting."

He climbed onto the bed then, making me shrink backwards as my face heated further. "I'm a demon. We have desires. Not only to eat but to crave. I have been craving, I am done with waiting."

"You just wanted my blood," I argued then.

His lashes lowered further. "Duchess... I did before, but I wasn't planning on drinking it. I had my doubts before... when you were so little. But... I never knew I'd fall in love with you all over again."

My lips thinned then.

"Duchess, I have been kind, I have served you. I have been patient." He gazed up. "Are you going to continue to resist me?"

I looked at his chest then, breaths straining as I tried to control this fluttering feeling inside. "You can kill me. In one second."

"I won't."

"You can change your mind."

"That hasn't bothered you before," he said then, smiling. "Why would you sign the contract with me then? You agreed to the terms long before you signed with me." He brushed my hair away from my face, making me gaze up. "Are you going to continue with these excuses? Or are you going to give in?"

My lips tightened then, and I watched him nervously.

"Duchess, what is wrong?" he said gently. "Are you not in the mood or something?"

"You're right," I said too quickly. "I am scared."

His eyes softened. "Why?"

"Because... because you're the only one who knows... what happened that night. And you're the only one who's cared for me. And... you're the only one who's seen me broken." I gazed up, iris beating in my exposed eye. "I don't want to get close to you, but I am *so* close. I lost everything that ever belonged to me. My family, my morals... my*self*. You are the only thing I've gotten close to ever since that night I vowed to never love again. I am cursed." I breathed shallowly. "What am I to do... when I lose you?"

Alistair just smiled, eyes glowing despite his sympathy. "Duchess, do you not have faith in me?"

"I never said that," I stated.

"You implied it," he said then, smiling. "You signed with me. I am vowed to protect you. Why would I leave you or let myself die without breaking the contract? Do you not understand the vow I swore to you?"

"I understand it plenty," I said then, raising my voice, "but I thought you died—"

"I asked if you had faith in me," Alistair said then, eyes still soft.

"I do," I said then, voice quivering slightly.

"Then you will understand that no one will take you from me. Your blood belongs to me still. Not for food anymore, but it is mine now." He lowered his face a little, raising his hand to slip under my eye patch. "No one can hurt you, no one will kill you, no one will take you. How can I protect you when I am gone?" He smiled as he tugged his hand upward, pulling off my patch and exposing my marked eye. "Everything I do is planned; it has a purpose. If I fake my death, I fake my death. But I will never truly die, I will never leave you." He ran his thumb under my marked eye, gently drying a tear. "There's no need to be afraid." He kept the smile. "You can trust me."

He leaned down and clasped his lips with mine, and I closed my eyes tightly.

I gave into him then, fisting his shirt in my hands.

But he just lowered his hand, down, down, under me, into me.

I let out a small whimper, clutching onto him tightly.

He separated his lips from me and set his forehead against mine. "Shhhh...."

He then started moving, pumping.

I let out soft cries, fisting his shirt tighter as the fire built deep inside.

"Does it hurt?" he said then, slowing his pace.

I shook my head, burying my face in his shoulder.

He sped up the pace then. "Ah, I see." He smiled. "You're just shy, aren't you?"

I breathed uneasily as he kept pumping, holding my face into his neck as I tried to remain silent so no one could hear.

"You're very shy, indeed," he said then, chuckling. "It's adorable."

"Shut... up..." I managed to let out. "Stop talking."

He just lowered his head to fit against the top of mine. "Yes, duchess."

He was silent then, holding me to him as I squeezed my eyes shut tighter.

It was coming again... that familiar feeling... that burning feeling.

It etched higher... and higher...

Oh, god.

I squeezed my thighs together, entire body clenching.

But it released, making me let out a soft cry as he held me against him.

My body spasmed, racking against him repeatedly as he kept pumping, letting it last.

I cried out then, not used to this feeling as my fingers bit into his shoulders.

"Shhhhh..." he cooed, trying to soothe me for some reason. "Shhhhhh...."

I settled down then, gasping when he pulled away, and I spasmed from under him, trying to breathe.

"Shhhhh..." he kept soothing, pulling my clothes back in place.

After a couple deep breaths, I was calm and relaxed, half-asleep, almost.

He pulled back then, face hovering inches above mine.

I gazed up at him tiredly, trying to speak clearly but my voice was soft. "You said... you were done... with waiting... Why did you... only do... me...?"

His lips curled. "I'm done with waiting, yes. But right now... I just want to touch my duchess. That's all."

"That's... all...?" I echoed.

He set his forehead against mine, smile widening. "For now."

"Duchess?" Maddox said from behind me. "What are we shopping for?"

I smiled. "Definitely not me. I have enough crap as it is."

I felt his eyes burn into the back of my head.

I just stopped at a store front and turned toward them. "This is a thank you. I couldn't have done any of this without the help of you four." I nodded my head. "All of you deserve a prize of some sort."

Scarlet and Cammie squished their own cheeks, and Maddox's eyes sparkled.

Carter tried to remain calm but failed.

"*Really?*" they all said at once.

"Why would I lie about that?" I said then, turning toward the store front. "I'm cruel but not *that* cruel."

I then walked in the shop, all of them following behind me.

It was a weapons shop, one with once side covered entirely with guns, and the other covered entirely with swords and daggers.

Maddox and Scarlet immediately squealed in excitement and rushed forward, catching weapons and examining them before moving onto others.

I just smiled, staying in place.

We went through a lot of shops after this, though... we went to a bakery full of cakes and tarts which made Cammie lustful, almost, and afterward, we went to Carter's favorite shop... a... bookstore.

Hey, I'm not one to judge, am I?

I walked in after Carter, and he immediately went to the adult romance section.

Of course... because... why not?

Seconds later, Carter rushed back toward us. "Duchess, duchess, look! A limited edition!"

He flashed me a magazine, and my eyes widened when I saw a picture of a half-naked girl onto it.

Alistair immediately covered my exposed eye, but my mouth was still parted in shock.

"Put that back," he said, annoyed.

Carter grumbled in annoyance and walked off.

Wow, protecting my innocence after you took it last night...? What is with you?

Ten minutes later, Carter was immersed in a conversation with the store owner about some book series he was interested in. They'd been talking for a while, it felt like.

I stood at the front of the store, gazing around before looking fully at Alistair. "All of them had their fun. Except for you. Do you want anything?"

He gazed down at me then, red eyes glowing slightly with the sky lights. "I am fine with what I have, duchess."

My lashes lowered, and I stared back forward. "Well, if you change your mind, then let me know."

He was silent for a moment, but then he gazed down at me. "Actually... if you really mean it. There is one thing."

"Oh?" I said then.

About twenty minutes later, we were in an alleyway, and my brow twitched in annoyance as Alistair knelt on the ground.

His eyes sparkled like a child as he pet a bunny on the ground, rubbing its little belly as it squeaked and squirmed around.

When he released it, it climbed onto him, up onto his hair and clutched onto him.

He then looked up at me, pointing to his head where the bunny sat, lightly gnawing his hair.

I glared when his eyes glistened with a "please?"

"Alistair..." I said, "no."

He gazed up, pouting. "But you said *anything*! And plus... I had to give all the other bunnies to a shelter. I want one of my own! They're just so fascinating creatures!"

I closed my eyes tightly, sighing heavily. "*Alistair, I am allergic.*"

"I can make sure it never enters your spaces!" he argued. "You know I will, duchess."

I gave him an annoyed look.

He just smiled and stood, the bunny still clutching onto his hair.

His eyes grew lustful as he tipped his head back, sighing as he ran his fingers through his hair, making a low groaning noise as he flipped it backwards. "It's very hot out today, don't you think, duchess?"

He started unbuttoning his shirt, making my lashes lower despite something burning deep below.

"Really?" I said as he shoved his chest forward, exposing his pecs.

He gazed up. "It doesn't work on you?"

I just coughed and turned around, covering my face. "God, you're such a whore."

He just stepped up to me. "Pleaaaaaaaase?"

I sighed and kept my hands in my face. "Fine," I said then, raising my head, "keep the fucking bunny."

He silently cheered, although I ignored it and started walking forward.

"So, it did work?" he said then, following me. "It usually does."

I just rolled my eyes. "No, it didn't, you idiot. I did say *anything you wanted*."

I glanced over at him then, finding his smile all fox.

I just stared back forward, cheeks burning. "Button your shirt. Now."

He made a surprised sound and listened, buttoning it quickly.

We then stepped out from the alleyway.

"Oh, duchess, hey!" Cammie said, dashing toward us as the others followed behind her. "I GOT ENDLESS CAKES!"

"I know," I said, laughing softly, "I was there."

They all stopped in front of us, gazing over at Alistair.

"Uh... why does Alistair have a bunny on his head?" Maddox said then.

"It's his bunny—" I leaned forward, immediately sneezing.

Alistair took one step to the side—distancing himself and the bunny from me—and I glared over at him. "Clean that thing."

His lips themselves looked like a cat's smile. He just nodded once, blinking. "Yes, duchess."

I just rolled my eyes and stepped up to the car. "You're way too happy. It's concerning me."

"My bunny is in bed," Alistair said then, glancing over at me as I sat on my mattress. "Is that everything you need tonight, duchess?"

I avoided eye contact and nodded, keeping my eyes trained to the bed.

He came up to my me and pulled back the sheets, and I got under them, feeling him draw them back over me.

He just stepped forward and bowed. "I bid you good night."

He then turned and left the room, closing the door behind him.

I stared at the door for a moment before I sighed and sat up, pushing the comforter off me.

I just caught a blanket from my pile of sheets and stepped over to the door.

I then exited my bedroom, lashes lowering while I made my way down the hall.

I finally stopped at a small doorway, and I pushed it open.

I just shut my lashes, feeling the wind dust my face.

But I stepped outside—on the upstairs terrace—and then sat down onto the floor of the deck.

After wrapping the blanket tightly around myself, I rested down onto the wood, staring softly outside as I breathed in the night air.

I watched as two bats flew across the full moon and skittering away, and I listened as the crickets chirped, the wind brushing branches of trees and bushes together... and the stars, the stars sparkling in the night sky.

A memory suddenly flooded my mind, an image of my mother sitting out here with me when I was ten or eleven. I had my head rested on her lap, smiling as she brushed her fingers through my hair.

My lashes lowered then, and I closed my eyes, letting myself slowly drift.

But I suddenly heard footsteps, a soft tapping of shoes against the hardwood in the house behind me.

I didn't want to move, though... I was so comfortable and warm... and all the sounds were so nice.

I felt like a child again. If I imagined my mother sitting here with me, comforting me like she always did... then I could believe it was real. Maybe for a couple minutes, right?

But the door of the manor closed, and the footsteps tapped over to me.

Arms were slipped under me, and I parted my eyes to find Alistair's expression masked.

He just lifted me and sat down, setting me in his lap seconds later.

I gazed up at him curiously, but he just pushed my head to his shoulder and covered me more with the blanket.

Did he know...? Did I ever mention this memory?

I just closed my eyes and snuggled my face into his neck, feeling him rub his hand up and down my arm as I let myself drift, once more.

To be continued in "*The Wonderland Show*"

Don't miss out!

Visit the website below and you can sign up to receive emails whenever Arianna Courson publishes a new book. There's no charge and no obligation.

https://books2read.com/r/B-A-ERCW-IGDGF

BOOKS 2 READ

Connecting independent readers to independent writers.

Did you love *City of the Dead*? Then you should read *Alpha Bane*[1] by Arianna Courson!

"You're dangerous and addicting; every part of you screams insanity... but you're like a ghost; something that I want to touch, but my hand goes right through you."
Selene:
I'm not normal.
No, I'm definitely not normal.

---

1. https://books2read.com/u/3nGEDR

2. https://books2read.com/u/3nGEDR

Most of the world doesn't know that werewolves exist, but I do. He thinks I don't know what he is, and he thinks I don't notice his eyes on me while I do my homework at the coffee shop, but I do.

Bane Johnathan is the most dreaded, attractive, dangerous alpha in the entire nation; girls swoon over him like millions of little night dancers.

But his eyes are always on me.

Something about me interests him, and I've noticed through the years that he feels some power over ignoring me when I come up to him, but I'm the one with the power.

He watches me, he can't stop; something about me captivates him, and I choose to ignore his stares even when it angers him.

I don't care if little old Bane is angry. Right now? There's something else on my mind.

There's a new pack out there; a pack of corrupted werewolves lingering through the woods and killing humans, and I know Bane knows something about it, and I can tell they're plotting something.

I need to put down my book.

It's time to go up and question him.

And boy did I regret it.

Also by Arianna Courson

Chronicles of the Enchanted
The Silent Kiss
The Silent Kiss
Lullaby: A Book of Enchanted Shorts

The Bane Saga
Alpha Bane

The Chained Saga
Quiet, Now
Quiet, Now
Be Still
Be Still

The Crave Saga
Crave

Chains
Secrets
Bloodless: The Entire Crave Saga

The Fallen Shadow Saga
Lily's Fallen Shadow
Jason's Angel of Storms
Silence Me
Silence Me

The Vendetta Saga
The Demon's Duchess
The Shattered Carnival
City of the Dead
The Wonderland Show
A Song of Darkness
Duchess of Death
Vendetta

Standalone
Obsession
Catch Me if You Can
Catch Me if You Can
Corrupted
The Eleventh Hour

About the Author

Arianna Courson is an author of young adult and adult fiction, specializing in paranormal, fantasy, and romance. She lives in Colorado with her fat kittens and four cute puppies. Despite her writing activities, Arianna also enjoys music, songs that inspire her work. She divides her time between writing, watching anime, and enjoying the great outdoors.

Read more at https://ariannacourson.wixsite.com/ariannacourson.